Summer Blood

C. PEARCE

authorHOUSE®

AuthorHouse™
1663 Liberty Drive
Bloomington, IN 47403
www.authorhouse.com
Phone: 1-800-839-8640

Published by AuthorHouse   02/25/2013

ISBN: 978-1-4817-8453-5 (sc)
ISBN: 978-1-4817-8454-2 (e)

CONTENTS

Part Four
Why We Fight

Prologue

Jessica Folds walked briskly that night. Or as briskly as a girl could in six inch high stilettos. The midnight air was cold and sharp and Jessica cursed herself for not bringing a coat. Still it had been worth it. The party had been so much fun. Even without copious amount of alcohol. Her friend Charlot had been right about the short blue dress. The boys couldn't stop staring. Jessica smiled as she remembered stealing a few kisses. But it was the kiss from Jason Ryder that she remembered best of all. He was such a stud yet that night he only had eyes for her.

Jessica was glad she was nearing home now as the cold air started to bite. She let her mind wonder back to the party one more time. That sexy slow dance with Trent, tasting his sweet lips. A smile crept across her face. But then a strange noise brought her back to reality. It almost sounded like a voice calling her name. Maybe it was just her imagination. Her thoughts running wild over Jason and that kiss. But she heard it again. "Jess" A low whisper just about audible. Jessica turned around and thought she saw movement in the shadows. For just the briefest of moments. She shook her head, there was nothing there. But Jessica couldn't shake off the feeling that she was being followed as she carried on home.

Dare she look behind her again. As if for some reason there would be no one there if she didn't look back. Then suddenly she could hear foot steps behind her. It was almost as if some one wanted her to know that they were there. Jessica stole a quick glance behind her. Although shrouded by darkness Jess was sure she could make out the silhouette of a man. Jessica started to run faster. But it was proving difficult in her high heels. Jess's only saving grace was the fact home was just a few hundred meters away.

At that moment the heavens decide to weep. The rain came crashing down hard and fast. Massive puddles began to form in the tarmac roads. Water ran into the drains like tiny rivers. And the rain soaked through Jess's dress, making it cling to her skin. With her skin soaked dress combining with her heels Jessica found it more and more difficult to run. Home suddenly felt like a million miles away and she could feel the stalker gaining on her. Tears began to form in her eyes and run down her already rain soaked face. Her legs tiring her feet soar from all the running. Could she push her self that little bit further. Jess tried to block out the pain and fatigue and drove herself on. Out of nowhere she felt a cold rush of air brush against her skin. It was almost as if something had swept right past her. Jessica checked behind her one more time. The stalker was gone. Had he given up. Maybe he wasn't after her at all? Maybe he went off in a different direction and was only making haste because he knew it was going to rain.

But as that thought ran through her mind, Jessica ran into something with a hard thud. Or more like some one. The collision wasn't enough to knock jess of her feet. But she staggered back to see a tall lean man in a dark suit and rain coat. The man stared at her with empty hollow eyes. In that second Jessica knew she was staring into death. A dark abyss were no one returned. But even worse was to come. As the man smiled and opened his mouth. Jessica could see two large fangs. Vampire and impossible were the only thoughts that crept into her mind. Seconds later those thoughts were replaced by panic and fear. Jessica wanted to flee. But she couldn't move. Was she frozen by fear. Or did this monster hold some kind of hypnotic power. Preventing her from getting away.

The monster reached out and grabbed Jessica's arm. He pulled her in close. He Stroked her long brown hair and then pushed it aside baring her neck. Jessica felt a sharp pain and then a slight tingling sensation as the monster sank his razor sharp fangs into the soft white flesh of her neck. Jessica soon began to feel weary. It was if all her energy was being sapped away. She felt weaker with every passing second. Her eye lids became heavy and she felt unable to support her own weight. Only the monsters support stopped her from collapsing. Soon there was nothing but darkness. Death had come for her and Jessica gave her self willingly. Peace at last.

PART ONE

Blood of the innocent

Chapter one

DI Summer Richards had been called out to inspect a particularly grisly crime scene.

The victim a young girl aged between eighteen and twenty one. Was found stripped naked and hanging upside down from a tree. Rope had been tied around the young girls legs and she had been hoisted up and hung from a branch fifteen feet in the air. Displayed for all to see, like a sick piece of art. Summer watched intently as Police and fireman struggled to cut the victim free, being careful not to let the body fall to the floor. As soon as the body had been cut free and lowered to the ground Summer walked over to investigate. Summer was aware of the male eyes watching her walk. As she made her way to the victim. The Female Detective was a very leggy Five foot six. Slim But curvy. That combined with striking good looks, fiery red hair and bright green eyes. Made for a very attractive woman. Summer had become accustomed to all the male attention. And would even admit she did little to discourage it. Like most women Summer enjoyed looking and feeling sexy. She would often dress in tight fitting clothing and heels. Her lips would be painted thick and red. A women shouldn't have to feel bad about looking good.

As Summer approached the body a uniformed officer offered her a pair of latex gloves. Summer took them and slipped them on. She then started to carefully examine the body. She found it strange that she couldn't detect any kind of bruising. There was also no evidence of a struggle. But something caught her eye. The girl had what appeared to be two puncher wounds in her neck. Summer moved round the body for a closer look and gently ran her fingers over the small wounds. They were definitely holes. Other markings around the neck area looked like teeth marks. *What the hell could of done this.* Summer thought to herself. An idea flashed in her mind but she dismissed it straight away. *Vampire's!? Come on Summer.* She told her self that's just *crazy thinking.* "Ok guys" Summer spoke to the uniformed officers. "When the pathologist gets here. Tell him I want a full report on my desk ASAP. We need to catch this sick son of a bitch and fast"

"Yes M'am" Came a reply from the Senior Officer. A Sergeant in his early thirties.

Without saying another word Summer took off the disposable gloves and threw them into a bin. She then proceeded to walked to her silver Audi TT.

A few hours later Summer was sat at her Bosses desk. DCI Adam Greenhorn. He was a young man for his position. Not even forty. But he was driven, intelligent and well organized. Summer also had to admit that he was pretty good looking. He had thick black hair with flecks of grey giving him a rather distinguished George Clooney look. He had a chiselled jaw and looked as if he spent a fair amount of free time at the gym. Adam walked into his office and undid the buttons of his suit jacket. Before sitting down opposite Summer. "I take it you have read the Coroner's report?" Adam asked as he picked up a file from his desk. "I have Sir" Summer replied candidly. "Though I am not sure what I make of it."

"If I am honest. Neither do I" Adam replied. "Two incisions on the neck. Body drained of eighty percent of its blood. All we know for sure is that we have a right physco on our hands"

"Could it be some sort of vampire wannabe Sir?" Summer said half joking.

"Either that or it is an actual vampire" Adam flashed a wry smile. "We need to find out who did this and apprehend them Before they kill again."

"You think we have a serial killer here then?" Summer asked.

"Almost sure of it. Don't you agree. I mean this is certainly the MO of a serial killer. Hell bent on showing the world what they have achieved. Like a cat leaving a mouse on the doorstep."

"That's very true Sir" Summer agreed. "But we have got no motive and no clue's. where the hell do we start on such a case?" Adam looked at Summer and sighed. "I guess we could go for a public appeal. A witness may come to light, with some useful information. Other than that I am at a loss right now."

"I think we should do that" Summer said. "As well as information we need to let people know there is a dangerous killer out there."

"Ok it's agreed I will speak to the parents. See if I can arrange a press conference. In the mean time I'm going to need you to interview some of the victims friends. See if anyone knows anything. You can conduct it at the collage if you like. Might be easer on the kids, if their in a familiar place." Adam paused for a second. "Although you may need to leave it until tomorrow thinking about it."

"Yes sir" Summer said with as much enthusiasm as she could muster. It was a necessary job. But not one Summer was going to relish.

Summer sat on her white leather couch in her rented apartment watching the news with her cat Isaac. The apartment block was brand new and so were all the furnishings. Giving everything a crisp and pristine feel. Summer kept her eyes on the TV as Adams press conference started to air. The parents talked about their lovely daughter and pleaded for any information on there daughters murder. Then the program went back to the news anchor. The press even had a nick name for the perpetrator. Labelling him the "Twilight Killer" after the popular teen books. Even though those vampires didn't actually kill anyone. Still can't let the facts get in the way of a good headline. The anchor then began to criticise the police for their apparent lack of progress into the case. "Like they know anything" Summer told Isaac. But he was no use the cat just purred loudly and looked up at her with his big green eyes. Summer rubbed Isaacs head before getting off the couch and walking into her kitchen. Like the rest of the apartment it was brand new. Decorated with fresh white tiles and containing all the usual mod cons. Including a dishwasher, electric oven that was barely used and a microwave. A stressful and tiring job that involved long hours. Left Summer with little time to do any proper cooking. The shiny white microwave was her best friend and most used appliance. Summer took out a pasta bake ready meal from her fridge freezer and shoved it in the microwave. She clicked on ten minutes on maximum heat. As her dinner warmed in the microwave, Summer gave Isaac his supper. A tin of premium cat food and a dish full of milk. "Enjoy" Summer told him as Isaac trotted up to his dinner. The Ping of the microwave went off and Summer took out her ready meal. Which looked surprisingly appetising and sat back down in her living room. Summer couldn't bare to hear any more about her case as she ate her dinner. So she began flicking through channels. In the hope of finding something to watch.

Summer woke up a good hour early that morning so she decided to use the extra time to have a good long shower. Summer closed her eyes as she lathered her long red hair and felt the warm water of the shower on her soft bronzed skin. Even though she was still in good shape she sometimes felt that time was catching up with her. That she needed to find a man and settle down while she was still youngish and desirable. But finding a decent man in this day and age was nearly impossible. Especially some one who would understand the job. Being a detective meant long hours, sometimes not even coming home at night. A lot of men and women for that matter are not able to cope with that. Couple that with the dangers of the job. Made finding a partner who would stick around hard work. Summer dried herself off and got dressed. She slipped on a pair of tight blue jeans. A white jumper and a pair of knee high brown boots. She had a bowl on cornflakes and a strong cup of black coffee. She would need it, as today she would be interviewing the kids that last saw Jessica at the party. Summer would be going straight to the collage this morning.

As Summer arrived at the collage grounds she saw what looked like hundreds of flowers and messages. All laid out around the gates and fence in tribute to Jessica.

This young girls death had obviously hit the whole community very hard. Summer made her way to reception along the very sombre corridors. Even though the corridor's where full of children making there way to class rooms and lectures. Summer imagined that normally it would be loud and full of laughing and joking. But no one felt like laughing today. "DI Summer Richards" Summer said to the receptionist At the desk as she held out her badge. "Ah." Muttered the receptionist, a well presented women. In her early fifties. She wore a smart white blouse and had her greying hair tied into a neat bun. A pair of bi-focal glasses hung on a chain around her neck. "You're here to interview the students" The receptionist continued.

"Yes" Was all the reply Summer could muster. She knew she was as welcome at the collage as wanted to be there herself. "The headmaster has got a room ready for you. Carry on down this corridor, turn left then it's the second room on the right. I have the list of students you need to see here. Anyone you want to start with?"

"Her closest friend please" Summer insisted. Summer knew that Jessica's best friend would probably have the most information. She would also be the most upset. Best get her over an done with as quickly as possible.

Summer walked into the class room and sat at the desk. It was pretty much how she remembered a class room to be. Small full of vandalised desks with names and initials etched into them. Cheap uncomfortable chairs. The only difference was the big white board that replaced the old black board. Summer didn't have to wait long before A girl with long blonde hair walked into the room. Summer stood up to welcome the young woman who was still visibly shaken and upset. "Hi I'm DI Summer Richards" Summer introduced herself as casually as she could. "Hanna Green. The blonde girl replied while trying to force a smile. "I know this is very difficult for you. Summer began. "But if you can tell me everything you can remember about the night Jessica died." There was a slight pause. As Hanna tried to compose herself. "It's ok. In your own time." Summer broke the silence.

"Ok" Hanna managed to say. "I will do my best. We all want to help as much as we can."

"I know you do" Summer said reassuringly. Hanna began to tell Summer about the party and everything Jessica got up to, that fateful night. Even telling Summer about the kiss with Jason and the other guys. "Did any of the guys get jealous seeing Jessica kissing other boys?"

"No" Hanna replied candidly "They all know it's a bit of harmless fun. They were all too drunk to notice anyway."

"What about Jason?" Summer asked. Did he follow Jessica home that night.

"Oh no. Jason stayed to the end. Jessica always leaves early. I didn't see anyone leave with her or follow her out. Hanna sniffed as she tried to hold back the tears. But they ran down her face against her best efforts. "Hey don't be afraid to cry" Summer whispered as she placed a hand on the girls shoulder. "it's better than holding it all in. I think we are done here now anyway. Thank you for your help" All Hanna could do to respond was to nod her head. Once Hanna had left the room. The next student was called in and several more after. Summer interviewed the other students. All their statements were consistent. Only a handful of students saw Jessica leave and no one saw anyone following her. DI Summer Richards was no better off than before she began the interviews. She still had no clue who the killer was and not a shred of evidence. It was hopeless. How in the hell was she going to catch the perpetrator?

Chapter two

It had been a long and emotional day. Interviewing all those students, Summer couldn't help but feel there pain. Jessica had been a popular and bright student. No one could understand why this had happened and who coud have perpetrated it. The reports that came back from the coroner's office hadn't helped Summers mood. They hadn't found much. Just a few strands of hair that they tested for DNA. But it came back negative. The DNA didn't match anyone on record. In fact the coroner stated he had never seen anything like it. Summer wasn't sure what she was supposed to do with that information. She needed to go home and run herself a long hot bath. So she could lie back, relax and wash the day off her. But Summer had a strong urge to go round and see her Mother. Summer often rang her Mum to speak to her on the phone but it wasn't very often that she actually went round to the house. But after seeing so much heartache she decided today was a good day to change all that.

Summer knocked on the red door of her Mothers terraced house. Her Mum Linda was Sixty one years old. She had lived on her own since her husband Don, Summers Father had passed away. Which was almost five years ago. He died of a heart attack at the age of fifty nine while watching his football team Tottenham Hotspur play Chelsea. At least he died doing what he loved most. "Summer!?" Linda exclaimed as she opened the door. "Is everything ok?" "Don't seem so surprised to see me" Summer replied as she walked past her Mum into the house. "And everything is fine. I just came round to see you" "Well I hardly ever see you these days" Linda scowled. "It's not too much to ask to see ones only daughter once and a while"

"I know I should come round more often" Summer confessed as she sat herself down. Her Mum still had the same old three piece suit from when she was a girl. Apart from being a little worn around the edges. It was pretty much how she remembered it and just as comfy. "But you know what this job is like. Somedays a hardly have time for myself."

"I know your job is hard on you. But it would help no end if you could find yourself a decent man to settle down with" Linda looked at her daughter sternly "When was the last time you even dated?"

"A long time ago, I know. It's not easy finding a nice guy who doesn't get an inferiority complex over the job I do. Or to find someone who can put up with the fact that I am at work so much. It's like the old cliché, I'm married to the job."

"I'm sure you will find Mr Right one of these days."

"I hope so Mum."

"Well just remember there is little joy to be found spending your life alone. Anyway do you fancy a cuppa?" Linda asked changing the subject to avoid any arkward silances. "I would love one thank's Mum" Linda got to her feet and walked into her kitchen. This was the place she spent more time than aany where else. Even if she had always hated that wood chip wall paper. But her late husband had always liked it. So now she refused to change it. Also many of her favourit picture's hung on the wall Don's and her's wedding picture. Summers School photos bringing back memorys that sometimes didn't seem all that long ago. She filled the kettle up just enough for too cups and put it to boil. "You still take two sugars love?" Linda called to the living room. "Just one please Mum" Came the reply. Moments later Linda walked back into the living room carrying two steaming hot cups of tea. "I'm sorry if you think I go on at you Summer" Linda sighed. I just want you to be happy."

"I know Mum" Summer smiled. "But I am happy. I do a fulfilling job. Chasing down bad guys and putting them behind bars. It's a good feeling knowing that I help make the streets a safer place for people to live"

"I know love and I'm so proud of you and you know your farther was very proud of you too. Summer smiled as she took a sip of her tea. She knew she was lucky to have such a caring and understanding mother.

It was getting late. Especially for someone who had work In the morning. But Robert Young had been celebrating a big win in the pool pub leagues. Maybe celebrating a bit too much for a work night. Roberts Team the New Eagles had beaten there opponents comfortable four games to one. With Robert winning his match very easily. Shortly after he and his three team mates had downed one or two pints too many. Now feeling tipsy he began the fifteen minuet walk back to his home. At least the alcohol in his system prevented him from feeling the autumn chill. *That's odd* Robert thought to himself, he could of sworn he heard a noise. Coming from just ahead of him. He stopped for a second and took a good look around. But there was no one there. *Must be imagining things.* He thought to himself as he carried on with his journey. But he heard it again. Only this time Rob thought he heard his name. Then he heard it again a low whisper fluttering in the wind. Calling his name. *Who is that* Robert thought. "Jenkins is that you" He called out angrily. Jenkins was one of Robert's team mates and friend's who was a well known prankster. There was no reply. Just the silence of the night. Robert decided to pick up his pace and hurry home. But some one stepped out of the shadows right in front of him. Robert stopped in his tracks. The figure of a man stood before him cloaked by darkness. Robert couldn't make out a face or anything. All he knew was the man was tall. Six foot, two at least. "Who are you" Robert stuttered. He had hopped not to show his fear. But fat chance of that now. "I am the new beginning that your kind has being crying out for" The man said in a menacing tone. "And you my friend are to deliver a message" "Who am I supposed to deliver this message to. Robert asked condescendingly. As his nerves started to turn into irritation.

"I'm afraid this isn't the kind of message you tell"

Robert swung his pool cue case as the man lunged forward. But who ever this man was. He was strong with quick reflexes. He caught the case easily in one hand. Tore it from Robs grip and threw it to the ground. Then In one swift motion the man grabbed Robert and pulled him close. Robert saw the mans bright yellow eyes. For less than a second he looked into them. He saw an emptiness. An emptiness that scared him more than his inevitable death. There was no emotion in the beasts eyes no hate, no love. He was hollow. As he struggled in vain to free himself from the monsters grip. Robert felt his head being pushed to the side by a large and strong hand. Then what felt like two large needles pierced his skin. Pain seared through Roberts body. But he could not move. He couldn't even scream for help. He just felt himself become weaker and weaker. Until he was swallowed up by the darkness.

Summer drove along the road toward the crime scene in her Silver Audi TT. Her favourite song Blue jeans, by Lana Del Ray was blearing out of the car stereo. Yet another murder to investigate. Her second in less than a week. "Prepare yourself" They had told her over the phone. This one is pretty screwed up. All murders are screwed up but she got the sense that this was going to be worse than the usual. Summer Pulled up and parked her Audi by a squad car. She stepped out of the car pulling out her long black rain coat and slipping it on as she walked towards the gathering cops. The open rain coat bellowed slightly in the gentle morning breeze, revealing her skin tight jeans and modestly cut top. That showed just a hint of cleavage. As she got a visual on the crime scene, Summer could see what they had been warning her about.

The victim had been literally crucified. The victim a young man. Who at first glance was in his early to mid twenties had been stripped naked and nailed to a make shift crucifix. Forensics where already there but had held off their investigation until Summer had seen the crime scene for herself. She really wished she hadn't needed to. As she took a closer inspection she could see that the victim had four six to eight inch nails hammered into him. Two through each wrist and two through each foot. Summer wondered if the young man had been nailed to the cross alive. She shuddered as she imagined the pain and sick images began to flood her mind. "I've seen some sick things in my time" Summer said to the chief mortician "But this takes the biscuit."

"I have seen this once before" The mortician Eric Von Wolfe responded. Von Wolfe was a well respected coroner and considered one of the top men in his field. At fifty six he had lived in London for over thirty years. But he still had a heavy German accent. I was ten maybe twelve years old. Living in Dusseldorf at the time. I remember it like it was yesterday. When your young like that these kind of images are burned into your mind. Took me years to get over it. But it's that incident that led to me choosing this carrier. But I remember the towns people at the time. They said that the victim had been drained of blood. Like the girl from six days ago" "You don't think this could be the same guy do you?" Summer asked quizzically. "he would have to be like seventy" "Nine" Von Wolfe replied. "But the similarities are striking. I will have to have him in my lab see what I can find out." "Ok get him down" Summer ordered turning her gaze away from the victim. She had seen all she could bare. Summer now wondered if Von Wolfe was on to something. Could a Murder over forty years ago in Germany have any connection with these?

Chapter three

Robert young lay motionless on the morticians slab. Waiting patiently to be dissected. Eric Von Wolfe snapped on a pair of blue disposable gloves as he walked round the table in his rather grey laboratory. The building itself may be old and the lab may be in need of a lick of paint. But it was all mod con's. Von Wolfe had everything he needed and more at his disposal. The fist thing Von Wolfe checked was the victims neck. As he expected there were two puncture wounds along the Jugular. The holes them selves where consistent with two rather large canine teeth. Impossible he thought. He didn't really click with the first victim. Maybe his subconscious wouldn't let him. His brain trying to protect him from the nightmares. But it all clicked into place. Eric remembered talks of vampires back in Dusseldorf. It was all nonsense of course. But was it. Von Wolfe couldn't ignore the similarities. Or the fact a Seventy year old man would never have the strength to nail a young man to a crucifix. It could be a coincidence. Maybe a copy cat. But something inside Von Wolfe told him it wasn't.

Eric took the scalpel. Spoke into his tape recorder and proceeded to cut into the dead mans chest. But a hand grabbed Von Wolfe's wrist. A startled Von Wolfe looked up to see the dead man's hand tightly squeezing his arm. The dead man sat up. Like a zombie or vampire from a horror film. "Jesus Christ!!" Von Wolfe Shouted.

"He won't save you" Robert hissed as he snapped Von Wolfe's wrist as if it were just kindling. Von Wolfe screamed in pain. "Are you going to kill me?" A terrified Von Wolfe asked as he glared at the abomination standing over him. "I really don't want to" The monster confessed "But I am so hungry" With that Robert grabbed the mortician and hoisted him up. With an angry look on his face and pure evil emanating from his demon yellow eyes. He drank the life force out of Eric Von Wolfe.

Harry Worthington sat on his black leather chair staring at an endless stack of paperwork that sat on his antique oak desk. Paperwork was a necessary part of the job. But that didn't mean he had to like it. Harry was in his sixtieth year he was balding but built like a brick out house and had a voice to match. It was booming and authorative. It often sent a chill down his subordinates spines. Which could be quite handy in his line of work. When Harry heard his private mobile phone ringing he was glad for the brake. But that was before he had heard what the man on the other end of the line was going to tell him. Harry riffled in his desk draw until he found the phone. Knowing it could be only one of five people he answered the phone. "Hello" his powerful baritones boomed down the line. "Sir" Came a rather skittish reply. I'm . . . . I'm afraid we have a situation."

"Well spit it out man" Harry demanded. He listened intently as the man on the other end explained what had happened and why he should be worried. "Damn it man" Harry bellowed. There was a large bang, followed by the rattle of cup's and stationary as Harry slammed his fist down onto his desk. "You said not to worry. That you could control them and now this happens."

"What do you want me to do Sir" The man asked nervously.

"I want you to do nothing. I will handle this myself. I can't afford anymore cock ups. If anyone finds out my hand was in this. I'll be out on the street!" With that Harry hung up and placed the phone on his desk. He sat in silence and pondered for a moment before reaching under his desk. He pulled out a small glass and a bottle of single malt scotch. He poured himself a shot and gulped it down. He then reached for his private mobile phone and pressed five on his speed dial.

Spencer slowly and carefully unscrewed the silencer on his Glock nine millimetre as he watched his target slowly die. The man he killed was in is early forties and worked for a major corporation. A corporation that was into some very dodgy dealings. The man that was lying on the floor drowning on his own blood was about to blow the whistle. Something the Chief executive couldn't afford to happen. So he called Spencer. Spencer was just a pseudonym. Not his real name. He had so many alias's he sometimes wasn't sure what his birth name was any more. But this kind of work needed a man to be many people. Needed a man to be ghost. Living in the shadows. Many names, many aliases many different lives. That's how he stayed ahead of the law. Today's job had been relatively straight forward. Spencer had spent the best part of the week on surveillance. Following and watching the target Studying his routines. From his habits and hobbies after work. Were he went. Whether straight home, to the gym or to a lovers and how long he stayed there for. Turned out the target liked to go straight home for at least an hour before going anywhere else. He would Shower get changed and eat some supper. The target couldn't go to the loo without Spencer knowing about it. Spencer planed the job to the last detail. So nothing could go wrong. At Ten past six precisely with gun in hand Spencer kicked down back door of the targets home. As he expected the target was in stood in the kitchen by the oven cooking his supper. Before the target had time to react or even open his mouth in protest. Spencer fired two shots into the mans chest. The target slumped to the floor struggling for breath. Normally Spencer preferred a clean shot to the head. But this job had to look like a botched robbery and not a professional hit. No suspicion could fall on his employer or his company.

Spencer slipped the unscrewed suppresser into one of the many pockets in his black combat trousers. Then he placed the Glock securely in its holster. Spencer stood and watched as his target struggled to breath his last breath. His lungs had been slowly filling up with his own blood. A horrible way to die Spencer had to admit but it was efficient. Spencer took no joy from any of his kills. But he didn't hate it either. He was just indifferent. As a former SAS Soldier he had seen so much death it didn't phase him anymore. This is what allowed him to do such a well paid job, that he found interesting and stimulating. Just to make sure the robbery scenario looked convincing Spencer started to ransack the house. Going through draws and cupboards and emptying there contents onto the floor. He decided to take some expensive looking trinkets that sat on a mantle piece in the living room. He also took the targets wallet that had been left on the kitchen table and relieved the man of his Rolex.

That should do it Spencer thought as he tucked the Rolex into another of his pockets and walked out of the house.

Spencer felt the soft vibrations of his mobile phone as he walked to his car. He pulled the phone out of his pocket and answered. The voice on the other end of the line was extremely familiar. A man he had done business with on several occasions. "I have a very sensitive job for you" The man explained in his heavy baritone's. "This is above Top Secret. I need you to understand that." "I get it" Spencer replied. "I will send you a flash drive in the usual way, to the usual place that contain all the information you will need. You will have one hour to look at the information and to absorb that it. After that the flash drive is programmed to release a virus into your computer. As I made clear. No one else can see this information. Carry out your tasks successfully and you will be paid five times your normal fee. I have already wired fifty thousand pounds to your normal account as a sweetener."

"Sounds good to me. I will be in contact soon" Spencer said as he hung up. For the first time in a long while Spencer felt uneasy. Something about this job stank. He could feel it already. But it was too much money to turn down.

Summer sat at her desk glaring into her PC. She was searching for anything she could find on the Dusseldorf incident, that Dr Von Wolfe had told her about earlier in the day. It didn't take Summer too long to find what she was looking for. Google was such a wonderful invention. Type in the right keywords and you could find anything you wanted in seconds. Summer clicked on what looked liked a promising link. Within seconds she was transported to a site that included a grainy picture of the crime scene. It certainly looked very similar to the one she had been at this morning. There was also a report under the picture. That luckily had been translated into English. It stated the date Nineteen Seventy Three and confirmed that the victim had been drained off all his blood. It also went on to describe that the victim had too small puncher wounds on the side of his neck. Which was consistent with victim number one, Jessica Folds. But she would have to wait until

Dr Von Wolfe's report before she could draw any comparisons with victim number two.

But as Summer read on she was surprised to find that this murder didn't make any of the national papers. In fact it only made it into one of Dusseldorf's local rag's. The report was written by a young journalist by the name of Henrich Muller. She clicked on the link to his wed page. Muller went on to talk about how the murder had been dismissed as nothing more than a hoax. That the body was said to have been a corpse that had been dug up and the nailed to the crucifix. Muller went on to suggest he suspect a cover up. That the government knew things that they didn't want the public to know. Of course Muller was written off as a paranoid conspiracy theorist and was turned into a laughing stock. This had forced him to flee Germany. Turns out he had been living in Manchester England for the last thirty years. *Maybe I should pay him a visit.* Summer thought to her self. There was a knock on Summer's office door. She quickly shut her laptop and turned to see her Boss Adam looking quite distressed. "Adam" she said as he let himself in "What's wrong?"

"It's Dr Von Wolfe. He has been found dead at the mortuary"

"My God!" Summer exclaimed "What the hell happened?"

"We have no idea. But that's not all. The body of the young man. Robert. Has just disappeared."

"How do you mean disappeared?" a stunned Summer asked

"Well you know. It's bloody gone. Stolen. I don't know"

"Why would some one steal a body?"

"No idea. There doesn't seem to be any witnesses and the CCTV footage has gone"

"Gone how can that be!?"

"No idea unless it is some sort of inside job. But I don't think there was anyone else there at the time. It's completely baffling I know. That's why I am sending you there to investigate. I want you to get yourself down there right away."

Down at the mortuary Summer was shocked to see Dr Von Wolfe's prone body lying lifelessly on the floor. See had seen plenty of murder victims in her time. But not someone she knew and had worked with. It seemed so surreal. Summer grabbed a pair of disposable gloves from a box she found sitting on a table. She put them on and started to inspect the body. Straight away she could see his right wrist was broken. As It was facing in such an unnatural position. She wondered how it could have been broken in such a way. Even though that was something for the new coroner to determine. Out of some sort of instinct born from the last two murders Summer checked

Von Wolfe's neck. As she expected there were two puncher wounds. Summer was convinced that the Coroner would discover that Von Wolfe had been drained of most if not all of his blood. A sudden thought came to summer's mind. Dr Von Wolfe's tape recorder maybe that had something useful on it. Summer started to search for the Recorder. But she couldn't see it any where. It wasn't on the table Or on the floor by the victim. Just in case she went through the deceased Doctor's pockets but came out empty. It just wasn't making sense. No Tape recorder and no CCTV footage. Someone else had got here first. A professional no doubt. Some one who had been ablbe to sneak and and out unseen taking any evidence with them. But for what purpose. Was this another cover up, like in Dusseldorf. What the Government know that they were so determined to hide.

Robert ran through the streets wearing only a long white lab coat and flat cap that he found hanging up in the mortuary. How the hell had he got there and why did he have an uncontrollable urge to drink that mans blood. Robert was disorientated and confused. The sunlight hurt his eyes forcing him to squint, this meant he could barely see where he was going. Not that he really knew. But some unknown force seemed to be driving him forward like an in built homing beacon. Robert could swear that as he past people in the street he could hear their hearts beating and the sound of their blood pumping through their bodies. He was also quite sure he could smell their blood. It smelt sweat, it smelt like food. Fortunately for them he had already eaten and wasn't hunger at this moment. Robert walked through another two streets. Doing his best to avoid people and keep to the shadows. Before going down a run down housing estate. He walked to the end of the estate to the very last house. He walked up to the front door and pushed on it. The door swung open and he walked in. Inside the house was pitch black. For the first time since he had re-awakened Robert could see properly. With the sudden clarity of vision came a clarity of mind. He knew what he was and he also knew where he was. The home of his new master the vampire who had made him. Everything was starting to become clear.

Chapter four

Spencer had finally retrieved the flash drive from his contact. As was promised it was in the usual place. A waste bin on the corner of Oxford street half a mile from Spencer's home. But before he could even make the short trip to collected it he had received another call. It was from the same contact. He needed Spencer to go down to a mortuary and "Clean up". Clean up removing any and all evidence of any crime or wrong doing. Spencer had managed to sneak in grab that mornings CCTV disc and the coroners tape recording. Which he then placed into a brown envelope and dropped into the same bin he retrieved the flash drive from. What a morning.

The first thing Spencer did when he switched on his laptop was to check his bank account. He had a special Swiss account that all the money he earned from special assignments was wired to. The Swiss were great. No tax and no questions, they didn't care where he was getting all his money from. It was a sweet set up. The money was there alright but it wasn't what he was expecting. There was an extra fifty Grand. They must of wired in a bonus for this mornings work. Spencer signed out of his bank account and opened up the brown padded envelop that contained the flash drive. He took the drive out and carefully placed it into one of his laptops USB sockets. Spencer was shocked at the information the drive contained. Certainly he was expecting something shady and possibly unusual but this!? If it wasn't for all the money he would have been convinced that this was some sort of wind up. But Vampires!? They aren't even real. Are they? But more to the point. Spencer didn't have any clue how to even go about killing vampires. Was it like in the stories or would a bullet do the job. I guess there was only one way to find out.

Summer drove into Manchester. It had been a long and frustrating drive from London. She almost wished she had taken the train instead. At least she could of chilled out and read a paper or even gone over some case files on her laptop.

After she had completed her investigation of the coroners lab. Summer had gone back to her office and had managed to find address details of one Henrich Muller. Summer had then decided to pop round unannounced. She was worried that if she rang him first it may have scared him off. Following the instructions of her GPS Summer soon found the street that Muller resided in. There was his house. Number Thirty four. Summer parked her car as near as she could and made her way to Muller's door step. As there was no doorbell Summer rapped the shiny brass door knocker three times. Moments later a man in his mid to late sixties answered the door. Summer smiled at the balding man that stood in front of her. He wore beige corduroy trousers and a dark green cardigan over a multi coloured striped shirt. "Mr Henrich Muller." Summer asked politely.

"Yes that's me" The rather confused Mr Muller acknowledged.

"Detective inspector Summer Richards" Summer told him as she flashed her badge. I have a feeling you may be able to help me regarding a murder inquiry."

"Then you better come in Detective" Muller said as he stepped to the side.

"You will have to excuse the mess I'm sorry" Muller apologised "Its not often I have visitors I'm afraid."

"Its quite alright" Summer assured him. She followed her host down a narrow, red carpeted hallway. The walls were covered in various art work and photos. Many of a gothic nature. Depicting vampires and other monsters. Some other painting hanging further down the hall seemed to show a great battle. Possibly of the crusade era. "Just through here" Muller instructed as he opened a well varnished wooden door. "This is my office" He announced before disappearing inside. Summer followed him into the room. "Please take a seat" Muller offered as he gestured to one of two old looking green leather arm chairs. As she sank into one. Summer was surprised at how comfortable the old leather chair was even if it looked like it had seen better days.

Muller's office was about the same size as an average sitting room. But unlike most peoples sitting rooms, this office was full of shelves. Each shelf was stacked full of very old and thick looking books. Which was probably how the room got its distinct musty smell. The room also contained an old fashioned fire place where a large coal fire roared healthily. It was almost the stereotypical office of a true English gentleman. Only spoilt by the fact the owner was German and the brand new laptop sitting on his pine desk. "I'm really not sure how I can assist you Detective"

"Please call me Summer" She interrupted. "Lets start with Dusseldorf Nineteen Seventy Three." With those words Summer could see the expression change on Muller's face, as his eyes narrowed suspiciously. "What do you want to know about Dusseldorf precisely?" The old man asked. Still sounding uncertain. Summer took out her smart phone tapped the screen several times and handed the phone to Muller. This picture was taken twenty four hours ago in London."

"can't have been" Muller said shaking his head. "It's just like it."

"Tell me" Summer insisted in her most seductive voice. "Tell me about Dusseldorf. It may be important."

"It was a summer afternoon" Muller started in his German accent. "I was a young reporter just starting out for the towns local rag. A friend had come across something early one morning while walking his dog. He knew I needed a brake and phoned me before the police. He obviously had a strong stomach. Because when I saw" . . . . The old man paused. ". . . . it I threw up almost immediately. I knew I wouldn't have long so I took a few quick photos and fled the scene. I developed the picture's and as I inspected them with a magnifying glass. I thought I could make out two puncher wounds in the victims neck. Later that week stories where being told about a vampire attack. Not only that but of demons living amongst us. But that's all it ever was stories. Any investigations on the case were closed and the whole affair was written off as a hoax. As I am certain you already know. But that didn't stop the towns people talking. Or the many disappearances that happened that year. Non of them investigated with any real intent. There are Demons living amongst us I am certain of that. While we own the day. They own the night."

As daft as that last line sounded. Muller made it seem very sinister, very real. "There's something else you should know" Summer said as she began to explain the events in the mortuary. "So the body just vanished without a trace." Muller repeated.

"You see vampires can transform a human being. Turn them into a vampire if you will. They drain a person of most of their blood. Then when you are near death they offer you their blood. You drink as you have no choice. The demon blood mixes with yours and a new demon is born inside a human shell. A demon we know as a vampire. It is said that a vampire will carry the memory's and personality of it's human vessel for many years. Maybe indefinitely"

"And how do you know this?" Summer asked not knowing whether to be impressed or horrified. "After what I saw I felt I had no choice but to dedicate my life to the research of demons. But I hit a brick wall. There was only so much I could find out."

"Why do you think that is" Summer inquired.

"History has its secrets. Some are long lost and forgotten. Maybe someone out there knows of these secrets maybe not. But if you want to know to fight these monsters I recommend you read a good book. Dracula for example. Many a good fact can be found buried in fiction."

"Thank you for all your help Mr Muller." Summer said as she got up. "You have been very helpful."

"Glad to be of assistance. Henrich also rose from his chair and showed the young detective out.

Harry arrived home from a busy day. His wife was still out with there youngest daughter. It was Tuesday so it would be dance practice tonight. One of few real joys in his life was watching his beautiful daughter on the stage. She moved with such poise and grace. Although as a dotting farther he may be viewing things with rose tinted glasses. But he was sure he was right. His oldest daughter Clara was at Cambridge.

She is so intelligent even more so than Harry himself. With her blonde hair and blue eyes she had her mothers beauty. He had really been blessed with such a beautiful family. Even he sometimes questioned the need of a mistress. But we are only animal's he would tell himself we all have needs. We all have our dark and depraved side's. Harry's mistress would do things to him and for him that his wife would never dream. Things Harry needed. It was cold evening which was just as well. As Harry wanted to start a fire. Harry hung up his coat in the cupboard then went into the kitchen and grabbed the fire lighters, matches and some lighter fluid just to be sure. He set some kindling and fire lighters in the fire place and doused them in lighter fuel. He then struck a match and threw it in. The fire started. Helped no doubt by the fluid. He let it burn for a few minuets before placing some coal onto the fire. I wasn't long before the fire raged. Harry took the brown envelope one of his aids had given him that afternoon. He opened it up and pulled out a disc and a small silver tape recorder. The disc contained CCTV footage that Harry Worthington didn't want anyone to see, ever! Harry threw both item's onto the fire and watched as they burnt. The fire cackled and spit as its flames embraced the two objects. Harry knelt down in front of the fire to warm his hands. He knew one day he would feel the fires cruel caress against his skin. Tongues of fire lapping against his delicate white skin as he danced the Devils dance down in hell. As long as his family never know the things he has done. Thing's he assured himself he had to do.

Robert was still unsure what he was doing in this old run down house. Or how and why he came to be here. But here he was non the less. It certainly looked like a vampires dwelling. All the windows were heavily boarded up keeping any light at bay. There also was very little furnishing, just a couple of old wooden chairs. There was no carpets and the wallpaper was peeling off all over place. "Hello anyone here?" Robert called out. But there was no response. There was something was going on here. Something wasn't quite right. Then it happened. All in a matter of seconds.

The front door came crashing in with a loud bang. Robert felt a sharp pain in his chest swiftly followed by fifty thousand volts pulsing through his body. Robert fell to the ground convulsing. He had never known such agony, not even as a human. As he spazzemed on the floor. Robert could make out four heavily armed men dressed head to toe in black enter the room. One of the men seemed to be shouting orders. But Robert was in far too much pain to make out any words. It felt like his whole nervous system was on fire. Then out of no where he saw another dark figure. Who or whatever the figure was the operatives couldn't see him. He took out the guy who held the taser gun and yanked the wires out of Roberts chest. Gradually the pain started to subside and his senses started to return. Robert heard the crack of bones braking and more shouting from the men in black as he tried to get to his feet. There was a blood curdling scream of pain and then another sickening crack of bones. By the time Robert was to his feet. All four men were on the floor, presumably dead.

The other creature in the room with him had stopped moving. By now Robert had worked out that he was another vampire. He wore a black suit with a blood red tie and wore a sinister smile on his face. "You knew they were coming for me didn't you?" Robert sneered angrily You where hiding here, waiting for them. I was just being used as bait to lure them out"

"Your quite right brother" The vampire admitted. His voice sounded almost inhuman. There was a deep rooted menace in there and a darkness. That you couldn't really explain but non the less you knew was there. "I had to lure the Special operatives here so I could take them out. And yes I used you for that very purpose. But look on the bright side your not dead and now we have uniforms and guns" The vampire smiled. "I'm Lucius by the way. Your maker, your sire if you like. that's why you came here. A new born vampire always has a strong connection to their sire. It's as if your programmed to find us. It's kind of like a built in survival code. The change from human to vampire can be very confusing at first. New born vampires often require help and guidance. Any way help me undress these guys and then we can get changed." With out a thought Robert felt compelled to do as he was told. Maybe that had something to do with the sire thing he wondered. The two vampires quickly undressed the operatives, disguised and armed themselves with their clothing and weaponry.

Chapter five
Two weeks later.

This was the one thing Summer dreaded most of all. She knew it would happen sooner or later. That it was totally unavoidable. The set up. A kind of blind date where a friend brings that "dreamy" guy from work to meet you. She could see the three of them at the table as she walked into the restaurant. Her best friend Kim her partner George and mystery guy she had never met before. Maybe she hadn't been spotted yet. Maybe she could make a run for it? Nope too late Kim had spotted her and was waving her over. Damn it. Summer thought to her self. Summer approached the table and pulled up a chair. "Hi" summer said forcing her best fake smile. "Hello Summer" Kim said mainly for mystery guy's benefit. Although now she was close she had to admit he was quite handsome. He had short but styled brown hair, soft blue eyes but a strong chiselled chin. He also looked very smart in a

crisp white and blue pin stripe shirt. "This is Spencer."
Kim introduced

"Nice to meet you" Summer smiled as she reached
to shake Spencer's hand. Summer than turned and
gave Kim her best death stare.

"The pleasure is all mine" Spencer smiled. "I take
it you weren't expecting me" he said picking up on
the look she gave her friend. After all reading people's
body language was an important part of his job.

"I'm afraid I wasn't sorry. I was expecting a girly
night out"

"No need to apologise" Spencer stressed. "It's
I who should apologise. I have to admit I was in
on Kim and George's evil plan all along" He gave
Summer a warm smile. Which she had to admit had
her feeling a little weak at the knees. So far Spencer
seemed quite the gentleman.

"I have been working with George for just over
two weeks now."

"he mentioned he was single" George interrupted
"And I instantly thought of you."

The four friends stopped their conversation
monetarily as a waiter came up to the table. He
took an order for some drinks and left a menu on
the table. Summer, Kim and the guys resumed their
conversation as they each took a look at the menu.

"When George told me bout Spencer I just knew
he would be right for you" Kim smiled as passed on
the menu to Summer.

"George kept going on about what a great girl you
are." Spencer told Summer. "Said I should meet you.

I told him I wasn't one for blind dates. But when he showed me your photo, I knew it was an opportunity I couldn't refuse. I don't have many rules in life. But one is to never turn down. the opportunity to meet a beautiful woman." Summer blushed. For the first time in a while a man had left her speechless and for all the right reasons. Handsome and charming. What was wrong with him? "I have to ask" Summer finally spoke. How's a catch like you single?

"I could ask you the same question" Spencer replied cheekily

"Touché" Summer giggled.

It had been a long time since Spencer had pulled the moves on a women like this. But he was glad he hadn't lost his touch. Or getting the job at Georges place would have been a complete waste of time. It was imperative to his mission that he got as close to Summer Richards as possible. He had to find out exactly what she knew about the murder's she was investigating. Did she suspect or know it was vampire's. If so what had she uncovered if anything and was she a threat to national security? Questions Spencer was confident he would have answers to very soon. "Kim tells me you're a Detective Inspector on murder"

"That's right. Tell the bloody world why don't you" Summer glared once again at Kim."

"It's not Kim's fault I kept pressing. When she eventually told me I realised why she had been holding out"

"It's fine I guess there's no harm in you knowing."

She couldn't be more wrong there. Spencer thought. "You must have a strong Stomach for that kind of work. There's no way I could do it" Spencer lied.

"Someone has to" Summer responded "I wish I didn't have to see some of the scenes I do. But it's a great feeling when you catch the bad guy." "I guess it all. All jobs have there up and down sides."

After what seemed like an eternity the waiter returned with the drinks. Two beers for the guys and a glass of red wine each for Summer and Kim. They ordered their meals before the waiter left the table.

Later that night after their meal and a couple more drinks. The quartet made their way down town to a trendy new bar. The atmosphere there couldn't have been more different from the calm of the restaurant. Loud music blared through the speakers. It was so loud that the four friends could hardly hear one another speak. Young adults in their late teens and early twenties moved and gyrated on the dance floor. While holding on to bottled drinks. It seemed like a world away to the four friends.

But if Summer didn't know any better, she could of sworn Spencer was trying to get her drunk. Every time she thought she had finished. She had another full one in her hand. At the end of the night Spencer asked Summer to go back to his house for coffee. Kim did her best to encourage her friend. But Summer politely declined the offer. Doing her best in her drunken state. To explain she was in the middle of an important case.

She really needed to sleep the night off I her own bed and be ready for work in the morning. Spencer gave Summer his mobile phone number and the four friends called for a taxi ride home.

PART TWO

The age of magic

Chapter six

Giles Price woke up early that morning. Straight away he could feel something was different. Something in the air was changing. He couldn't explain how or why, but things were about to change forever. Powerful forces both good and evil were shifting for the first time in a millennium. He could feel it in every fibre of his being.

Now was his time. This is what his farther had trained him for. For all those years. As his farther had trained him and his father's farther and so on. Training and knowledge that had been passed down his family for generations. Quite possibly centuries. "How will I know the right time to use this knowledge, if I even need to use it at all." He had asked his farther.

"When the time is right you will know" His farther had responded. It was the same answer someone tells you when you are looking for love. The right girl will come along they say. You will know when you find the one. Of course it all sounds like complete balderdash at first. But then you find her and all of a sudden it all makes sense. You know she is the one. A feeling everyone gets but no one can ever really explain. That's how Giles Price felt right now. Now all he had to do was find the Demon hunter before it was too late. they wouldn't yet know there true destiny. Only he could reveal the truth and show them the way's of the hunter. As his fore fathers had shown other's in the past. It would take Price hours to prepare the necessary spell to locate the Demon Hunter. After all he would be using spells that hadn't been cast for over a thousand years.

Acre 1291

The night air filled with the sound of war. The sound of steal clashing against steal as swords collided and the battle cry's of warriors. Blood was being spilt, flesh was being ripped and torn apart. As to warring sides fought to the death. The enemy were far stronger and faster. But they were becoming over whelmed by the sheer number of their opponents. Long ago they had called themselves The Templar Knights. But they were not Knights. They weren't even human. Summer knew this as she led her army of Muslim Saracens across the holy land, upon her trusty white steed. The Templar Knights exploded into clouds of dust as they were decapitated in battle. They would storm the fortress of Acre. The place the Vampires had made there base. No more would these demons hold Kings and Popes to ransom over loans. Under this disguise of Templar Knights and the veil of a holy quest. The vampires had amassed a vast fortune. A fortune they had used to bring Kings to there knees. Now was the time for this to end. Summer was descended from a long line of demon hunters and had been summoned by the Pope himself. He had given her this holy mission, destroy the vampires posing as Templar Knights.

The advanced guard of Muslim Saracens had already breached the fortresses defences as Summer on her steed galloped up to the huge castle. Beheading and trampling several vampires along the way. Summer's main mission that night was to locate and slay the vampire king. Who she believed was holed up inside the temple. Using huge battering ram that had once being a tree. Thirty of Summers men smashed against the massive wooden doors of the fortress with a huge battering ram. Eventfully the doors conceded defeat and came crashing down. Landing and crushing dozens of vampires that stood in wait. But many more came rushing out. Luckily numbers were still on Summer's side and many more men were now making their way to the fortress. Summer pulled on the reins of her horse and bolted through the massive entrance, where the two once sturdy doors had stood.

As she raced into the main hall she could see the vampire king sitting lazily on his throne surrounded by guards. The king was a strange abomination. So old he had started to look more demon than human.

His skin had become gray and leathery his eyes red and his ears pointed. His face was almost bat like in its features. *Was this what a true demon looked like?* Summer dismounted her horse and the kings guards attacked her. Six of them all coming towards her at once. But they where no match for her. Summer was too fast too graceful. She didn't just fight she danced. Moving around the vampires like lithe ballerina. Summer danced around the vampires attacks. Two vampires even ended up striking one another as they both missed their intended target. As they did Summer who wielded her sword like it was an extension of her own body. Beheaded the two demons. They both exploded into clouds of dust. She killed three more Vampires with similar ease and looked up to see a sixth running for his life. His king screeching at him to return. But his screams were in vain.

Now it was just Summer alone in the great hall with the King of all Vampires. He stood from his throne his black robe's draping onto the floor. He looked at Summer and smiled a wicked yet confident smile. In less than a heart beat he moved across the room and had the young vampire hunter by the throat. Lifting her clean off the floor with one talon like hand. "You dare challenge me" The ancient vampire hissed as he tightened his grip. Forcing Summer to drop her sword as she struggled for breath. Summer tried in vain to struggle free. But this vampire was strong. Far stronger and faster than any other vampire she had faced before. The king sneered at Summer and then through her across the empty room like she was nothing but a rag doll. Summer sailed threw the air and landed with a huge thud. Summer tried to pull herself up. She was shaken and hurt. But at least she was still conscious. Unfortunately she was also completely out matched. The old vampire now sauntered across the room like he had all the time in the world. He also had Summer's sword in his hand. "You can die by your very own weapon" he taunted. "A fitting end to a foolish girl" The vampire King raised the broad sword high over his head, ready to drive down hard into Summer's heart. But at that moment there was a loud battle cry as Summer's men stormed into the great hall. Distracted for half a second by the commotion the vampire King hesitated. It was all the time Summer needed to drive a wooden stake into the vampires heart. The vampire king screamed in shock and agony and then exploded into a cloud of dust.

Summer jolted up right in bed. Whoa what was that she thought to herself as she rubbed her neck. She knew it was a dream but it felt so real. She felt as if she had been whisked away to another country and time. Felt as if she had dealt and received every blow. Boy did her neck feel soar. Summer had never had a dream like that before. She climbed out of bed and walked to the bathroom in her Danger Mouse PJ's. Poured her self a glass of water and took a couple of small sips. At least her throat felt ok now. Summer took a couple of bigger gulps before returning back to bed. A quick look at her clock revealed it was nearly three am. Plenty of time for some more sleep before work. Hopefully no more night mares, this case must be affecting her more than she thought.

Three hours later the detectives alarm sounded. A weary Summer reached an arm over and hit the snooze button. She didn't know why she bothered. In another five minutes the same annoying sound would be ringing I her ears, telling her it was time to go to work. After two more hits on the snooze button Summer finally dragged her ass out of bed. At least she had woken in her own bed. Spencer had asked her back to his place for a coffee but Summer was convinced he had wanted more than that. As nice as Spencer seemed that was a road she wasn't prepared to go down just yet. Especially with a man she hardly knew. Summer walked into bathroom and switched on the shower. Waited a few moments for it to reach optimum temperature, before stripping off and steeping in. She lathered her self up with shower gel and she let the warm water saturate was it off her silky smooth skin. Summer stepped out of the shower and dried her self off with a fresh white towel. Wrapping the towel around herself she walked into her bedroom. Time to choose an outfit for the day. Summer felt good about herself after last night. She even felt sexy. So that's how she would dress. She slipped into a pair of skin tight black jeans a blood red top which showed a little more cleavage than usual. She completed the look with a pair of black knee high boots and her long black rain coat. Which had become like her trade mark. Today she was going to turn heads and she didn't care what anyone thought or said.

Spencer was feeling slightly irritated. Things had not gone precisely to plan. He had wasted precious time infiltrating George Whites work in order to get close to DI Summer Richards. The women he knew was the lead detective in a high profile murer case. A case that was heavily linked to his own investigation. Spencer had even managed to secure a double date with Summer through George and his partner Kim. But even though he had made headway flirting and using his charm. She refused to go back to his place. Too much a lady. Too sensible. He had to give her credit for that. But now he was back at square one. He needed to know exactly what she knew. His employer made it clear he didn't want her or anyone else finding out too much. Spencer had also hopped she might of led him too the vampire. Or at least revealed some clues that may of helped. But nothing. Harry Worthington wasn't a patient man. Spencer would have to employ a different tactic to complete his mission. He opened up his wardrobe and looked through many different outfits and disguises. Before finding what he was looking for. Spencer pulled out a neat navy blue suit and laid it down on his king sized bed. A bed that had seen many conquests. After killing recreational sex as his favourite hobby. He opened a draw by his bedside. He pushed on a secret panel and lifted it out. Underneath was a stash of fake Ids. Spencer riffled through them until he found what he was looking for. *Yes this will do* he thought to himself. *She will hate me for this. But she will respect the badge.*

Six weeks ago

Alarms sounded as Lucius walked down the white corridors dragging his hostage. His arm wrapped firmly around the scientists neck. Some fool had failed to implement all the necessary security procedures. Leaving several cells unlocked including Lucius's. The vampire had to wonder what else had been set loose, if he wasn't a priority. Still the lack of action in his direction was allowing him to make his escape. But getting out of his cell was only half the job. He still needed to escape the facility, which no doubt was deep underground. But that's where the scientist he had taken hostage would come in handy. He had already forced the man to tell him where to go and use his security clearance to get through several doors.

Lucius could hear the screams of dying men as he reached the facilities lift. A lift that required a retinal scan to be activated. The vampire shoved the scientists face into the scanner. It read the mans eyeball and activated the lift. Not a moment too soon as Lucius could hear footsteps running down the corridor. Using the scientist as a human shield Lucius span round. The S.W.A.T team froze, unsure of what to do. The vampire took advantage of their uncertainty and threw his hostage towards the operatives. The Scientist sailed through the sir and landed on the operatives. Knocking them down like skittles on a bowling lane. By the time they had picked themselves up the vampire was long gone.

Back in the present day Lucius watched coldly as Robert's body disintegrated in front of him. The young vampire had outlived his usefulness and was now just dust in the wind. He didn't need the inexperienced vampire slowing him down right now. Soon he would sire more vampires and create an army, to do his bidding. Turning only the most intelligent, most battle hardy as well as the rich and the powerful. He would make sure he had soldiers in key potions, in military and government. He would take over from the inside slowly patiently. By the time anyone realised what was going on it would be too late. Vampires would have already won. The time of vampires skulking in the shadows will soon be over. They would be the new rulers of this human infested world. But it wasn't time for that yet.

Now was the time for revenge. Five long years he had spent being the humans prisoner. Trapped in a cell like an animal. Used as guinea pig in various experiments. Experiments that were tantamount to torture. But Lucius had also heard things. Whispers down the corridors that they thought no one could hear. They talked about a patient Zero and her special blood. That had led to an amazing breakthrough, that could change human life forever. Breakthroughs that Lucius hoped could be used to his advantage.

Harry was feeling soar, after a good session with his mistress Veronica. She was a tall elegant beauty, with long Raven hair, tanned skin. She was thirty two years old with no inhabitations. Fun, sexy, dirty and a knock out in black latex and thigh high boots. Most nights after a session with Veronica. Harry would feel guilty. He new he shouldn't cheat on his wife and lie to her and his two daughters. But tonight he was glad for the release. Get rid of some tension and forget about his worries for at least an hour or so. He loved at bit of S&M. Being tied up and wiped was his favourit fetish. But unfortunately on this occasion it wasn't long until his frustrations returned. The vampires were still on the loose. The special ops team he had dispatched had all being found dead at a abandoned house. Obviously they had been no match for the demons. At least he had been able to send a clean up crew to remove the bodies and sweep the area for incriminating evidence. Before any one else discovered the scene. The last thing he needed was the police being alerted and snooping around. Harry was also annoyed that Spencer his number one guy hadn't been in touch. heard from. Harry had to be certain that nothing could be traced back to him. So far he had covered his tracks well. But one couldn't be too careful. One slip up and it could be game over. This current situation was heading dangerously close to that scenario. All loose ends needed to be tided up. That included Professor William Snyder. Snyder was the lead scientist, on the research they had been conducting and obviously knew too much. He would have to be taken care of before he could talk.

Back at home Summer was feeling exasperated. There had been no new leads on the case. She still had no clue who had perpetrated the killings of Jessica Folds, Robert Smith or Doctor Von Wolfe. She had no hard evidence to explain how a dead body seemingly vanished into thin air. All she did have was her own theory's. Summer knew that If they didn't find something concrete soon, the case be would put on the back burner. Or even closed down completely. Despite the evidence in put in front of them no one wanted to believe the killer was a vampire. Or they wouldn't let themselves believe it. If the government wasn't trying so hard to cover things up maybe Summer could of made some headway by now. She just had to hope that if the killer struck again he would get careless. Make that vital mistake that would lead to his downfall.

Summer was also annoyed that Spencer had given her a wrong number. Every time she tried to text or call it said number no longer active. What the hell was his game? Summer made herself a cup of mint flavoured hot chocolate and snuggled up on the sofa with her cat Isaac. "At least there's one man in my life who won't let me down" She said as she stroked and petted him. Summer picked up the remote control for her television and switched it on. As usual there didn't seem to be anything decent on.

Maybe if she flicked through the channels long enough she would find something worth watching.

York 1772

The cold air cut across Summers face as she rode her horse at a fast sprint. She knew she didn't have much time. An hour ago Summer had tracked down and killed a gang of vampires. The trouble was the vampire she was after wasn't with them. As she beat down the last of the vampires and made ready to slay him he gave her a warning. "He's going to your house." Summer quickly dusted the vamp before mounting her steed and racing home. She had to get there first. She had to stop him.

She stopped horse outside her log cabin home. That sat in the middle of the dense forest. As Summer ran inside she realised she was already too late. Her five year old son lay dead on the floor, near the doorway. His tiny neck had been twisted round and broken, snapped like kindling. Summer crouched over her the little boys body. Tears streaming down her face as she cradled his head in her arms. As she looked around the room she couldn't see any sign of her daughter Darla. "Please God tell me she got away" She said aloud. As she searched for her little girl she found her husband slumped in his chair. He was dead, two puncher wounds in the side of his neck. The vampire had drank her husband dry.

But where was her daughter? "Darla!" she shouted one more time. This time Summer received a response. A timid little voice coming from the back room. "Mummy is that you. Has the bad man gone" The little girl asked as she walked into the front room. "Oh my goodness thank God your still alive" Summer felt so relieved. At least the monster hadn't killed her little girl. As Ellie walked towards her Mother Summer met her and wrapped her arms around Ellie. But something was wrong. Ellie's skin was so cold. She touched Ellie's forehead and stroked her long red hair. The vampire hadn't killed her, it was far worse than that. He had turned her. Sired the little girl into a vampire. Despite what Darla now was Summer held her even tighter. "I want you to know, your Mummy loves you so very much" Summer sobbed. "Your not going to hurt me are you Mummy?" Darla asked innocently.

"No I won't hurt you baby. I promise I won't. You here me I won't her!" Summer screamed at the doorway.

"But you have no choice" Came the familiar voice of Lucius. Also known as Lucius of the Fall. The vampire leader Summer had been hunting for months. He had cut a bloody swath across half the county, killing dozens of people. Now though he was just playing games.

"Are here to kill me" Summer asked still clutching her young daughter.

"Why kill you. When it is far worse to let you live and suffer. You will live out the rest of you day's knowing that you couldn't save them. Their faces will haunt you forever. Your son your husband and the little girl you killed with your bear hands." Darla pushed her self out of her mother's embrace. Her face now I its true demonic visage. "Mummy I'm hungry" Darla said her voice still as sweet and innocent as ever. "Please" Summer begged as she looked at Lucius "Please just kill me" "Tonight there will be no more death" Lucius said coldly as he walked out of the house.

Summer sat up in a cold sweat. She had fallen asleep on the couch in front of the TV. Another one of those strange dreams. Where it felt as she had been transported into different time and living someone else's life. Just like the dream se had the other night. Where she killed the vampire king. This dream had also felt so real so visceral What was happening to her? She suddenly felt like she was missing something. That she was incomplete somehow. Were the dreams trying to tell her something?

A vampire never forgets a scent. Lucius certainly didn't especially the scent of someone who had practically tortured him on a daily basis. And like a dog a vampire was able to sniff someone out from miles away. Lucius's nose had led him here. To a large detached house in Chelsea London. The front garden was immaculate. The lawn was expertly manicured and the hedgerows were preened and pruned to within an inch of their lives. With flowers of spectacular colours growing in and around the borders. A one year old Aston Martin sat proudly in the drive way. Who new what vehicle was deemed precious enough to live in the garage. It would seem that Professor William Snyder had done very well for himself. Lucius began to look for a way in. Unlike common folk lore and legend a vampire didn't need to be invited to enter a persons home. Lucius sometimes wondered who cooked up such nonsense. But such misconceptions could easily play into a vampires hands.

It would be so easy for Lucius to use his strength right now and kick the door in. But that would make too much noise. Alerting too many people to his presence. The last thing Lucius wanted was someone alerting the police. No a more stealthy option was required. He checked the front of the building no obvious way in here. Keeping to the shadows Lucius made his way round the back. Another nice garden complete with a rather large fish pond. Snyder and his wife were obviously proud gardeners. A lack of security around the fish pond also suggested they had no children living at home. Lucius shifted his attention to the house. He could see a bedroom window had been left wide open. It Probably belonged to the master bedroom. That would be his way in.

Lucius jumped up and through the open window. Landing, as he suspected in the master bedroom. The walls of the room were painted in a deep red, with matching carpet and curtains. A huge king sized bed sat prominently in the centre of the room.

The occupiers of the house were no where in sight. But the warm glow of a bed side lamp suggested someone would be coming to bed soon. Lucius knew just where to hide. He took position behind the open door. This would keep him long enough to surprise his victims and then trap them in the room. The vampire stood motionless as he heard approaching footsteps. The sot sound of the footsteps inicted it was a female that was about to enter the room. Most likely Snyders wife. Hopefully her husband wouldn't be too far behind. Lucius stood silently in his hiding place as Mrs Sara Snyder entered the bedroom and sat on her bed. She was tall and thin her blonde hair tied into a bun. Even from where he stood in the dim light. Lucius's could see the tell tail signs of cosmetic surgery around the woman's face. It was mostly around her eyes with some laser surgery to remove some wrinkles. She was probably in her fifties. But to the human eye she looked early forties. She got off the bed and walked over to the window shaking her head. She closed it up and turned around to face Lucius, on the other side of the room. He stepped out from his hiding place in full vampire face straight into Mrs Snyder's view. She let out a scream. Lucius gave the women a stern look and pressed his finger to his lips. Instructing the women to keep quiet. She did as she was told. Sitting back on her bed shaking and taking deep breaths. Trying hard to keep her breathing under control. "What is it?" Came a William Snyder's concerned voice. "Don't tell me its another spider." He joked as he walked briskly into the room. He turned around sharply as he heard the door slam shut. Lucius gave him a sinister smile. intruder. "You!" Snyder exclaimed. Recognising the intruder straight away. "Are yo . . . . you here to kill me" The professor stuttered. His voice laced with fear. The vampire said nothing. He just continued his evil glare. The professor took several steps back not once taking his eyes of the vampire and sat down by his wife. He slipped his hand into hers and held it tightly. "Do you know this man" Sara asked feeling slightly confused.

"Yes" The Professor answered. There was little point in lying. Considering he was about to die and it was obvious to his wife that he had recognised the intruder. "What . . . . what's wrong with his face?"

"Oh come on" Lucius sneered. "I'm sure you can work it out."

"he's a vampire." William answered for her.

"And your husband is bad man." Lucius said. "Tell her what you did to me."

The question was met with silence. "Tell her!" The vampire repeated raising his voce just a few decibels. It was enough to encourage the desired affect. Professor Snyder turned to face his wife, tears rolling down his face. "We preformed experimentes on him and others like of his kind. Some of the things we did would constitute torture if done to another human being." His wife snatched her hand away. "I'm so sorry" Snyder snivelled. "They were things we had to do to make significant breakthroughs in medical science." Sara refused to look at her husband.

"Listen I know you were only following orders. Tell me who was in charge."

"Why should I" the professor asked "you are going to kill me anyway."

"Because it will determine how you both die. Quickly and painlessly or slowly and painfully. Snyder looked at his wife who now was crying.

"What have you done William. What have you done." Once more she looked away. "Please the professor begged leave my wife out of this and I will tell you everything you want to know."

"Very well" The vampire responded.

"The man who sanctioned your capture and the experiments you were subjected to. The man who had complete authority over the entire operation is Harry Worthington, the Prime Minister."

"Thank you" Lucius smiled. "That wasn't so hard now was it" In the blink of an eye the vampire moved across the room and grabbed Sara Snyder. William could do nothing but watched in horror as the vampire snapped his wife's neck. The sound of bones braking was sickening. "But you said . . ."

"I lied" The vampire interrupted. With another swift movment Lucius grabbed the balding professor and sank his fangs deep into the mans neck. But the vampire didn't intend to kill the Snyder. He had much grander plans than that.

It was nine am Monday morning and Summer was back In her office. Her case was now just days from being closed. It also seemed like Spencer had vanished into thin air. Kim had informed her that George hadn't seen him at work. Apparently he posted in his notice and never came back to work. It was almost as if Spencer had never existed . . . A knock on her door disturbed Summer from her day dream. She turned her gaze to her office door to see a uniformed officer waiting outside. It was officer Vardy, a tall stocky man, with short blonde hair and a goatee beard. "M'am there's a man here to see you" Vardy explained as he opened the door. "His name is Giles Price says he has important information for you. He's waiting at the front desk" "Thank you Officer Vardy." Summer wracked her brains. She couldn't remember a Giles Price. Who the hell was he and what did he know? Oh well only one way to find out. As Summer Richards approached the front desk she saw the man she assumed had to be Giles Price. He wore a sharp and well tailored grey suit. He was clean shaven, with greying brown hair. Price wore designer spectacles. Probably Gucci or Hugo Boss, he looked to be in his late thirties. Possibly early forties and he carried a black leather brief case in his right hand. "DI Summer Richards." The detective introduced her self and extended an arm.

"Giles Price" The man said as he took her hand to shake it. His voice was smooth but authoritative. Like an English stage actor performing Shakespeare. "Do you mind if we go somewhere else to talk. I don't feel entirely comfortable here"

"Sure" Summer agreed. There's a coffee place just down the street"

"That will do nicely" Price smiled.

Giles Price and Summer Richards sat at their table with too large Latte's. "So what's this information have you have for me" Summer asked as she tore open a sachet of chocolate sprinkles and emptied the contents onto her Latte.

"Straight to the point" Price smiled. "I don't want you to get the wrong idea here" He warned. "This isn't about a case. But it is important information regarding your self. Summer looked a little worried now.

"What is it then" She asked in a don't mess me around tone of voice.

"Well. How can a put this" The sharp suited man struggled with his words. "Your gifted" He finally said.

"Gifted" Summer repeated. Looking a combination of confused and pissed off. "Let me get this right you brought me out here. Taking me away from an important case to tell me I'm gifted." Summer stood up to leave.

"Wait I can help you. I can help to explain the dreams."

"What about my dreams" Summer said as she gave the man a stern glare.

"If I am correct you will have started to experience dreams of a very realistic nature. Probably involving yourself engaging in great battles. Battles that took place hundreds of years ago."

"How can you possibly know this" a stunned Summer snapped.

"There not dreams" Price continued. "Part of you probably realises this. You are reliving memories of your ancestors."

"You're off your rocker" Summer said as she started to leave "Just stay away from me"

"I will be right here waiting for you" Price called out after her. He wasn't sure if she heard him. But in all fairness the meeting had gone about as well as could be expected.

Chapter seven

Summer arrived back into the station only to be met by officer Vardy. Don't take your coat of M'am the officer warned her. There's being another murder. MO matches your case. The Victim was killed in her house in Chelsea. Forensics are already on there way." "Ok I will get down there now." At the Victims house Summer was met at the door step by two uniformed cops. "Upstairs, second room on the right" The older cop informed her. Summer walked past them and up the stairs. Dr Von Wolfe's understudy Kay Hardy was already there. "I had a quick look at the body" She told Summer "But I won't be able to do a thorough examination until I get the corpse in the mortuary." The young pathologist was a strange girl. Exceptionally bright and pretty. But when she wasn't in her white disposable cover all. You could see that her arms and neck were covered in a variety of tattoos. She also had several piercings including one in her bottom lip, tongue and rumour had it through her nipples. She wore her hair in a sleek bob that was died jet black and often wore bright red lipstick. That was thickly applied. But she was very good at her job and carried high praise from her former boss. "This house is registered under two names. A William and Sara Snyder. Do we know the whereabouts of My Snyder?" Summer asked as she rounded the bed to get a good look at the body.

"No one has been able to find or get in contact with William Snyder" Kay explained

"Ok. We can mark him down as a potential suspect. What can you tell me about the deceased?" Summer asked.

"Looks as if her neck was broken. Twisted round with bear hands I would say. She also has bite marks on the side of her neck. Matching the M.O of our vampire killer. I would estimate time of death to be between One and four am this morning."

"What kind of animal does something like this" "What you should be asking is what kind of animal sneaks in and out of a house undetected." came a familiar sounding male voice. Kay and Summer looked around to see a man in a navy blue suit standing in the door way. "Spencer!?" Summer blurted out in surprise. "What the hell!" "Spencer Smith MI5." He explained as she held out his badge.

"You're a bloody spook!" Summer sounded pissed off.

"That's one way to put it" Spencer smiled. "What was going on the other night. Are you spying on me?"

"I have been yes and I make no apologies. You know the job. The things we have to do at times. This is a very sensitive case. Involving nation security. I was hoping to find out what you knew, if anything. But you decided tom play hard to get." "Bastard!" Summer cursed.

"Look we haven't got time for this" Spencer's tone was serious. "We have a serial killer on the loose. Quite possibly a kidnapper as well. Shouldn't a William Snyder be here.?"

"What do you know about William Snyder" Summer demanded.

"More than you it would seem" Spencer gave a smug style. But quickly removed it when Summer glared at him disapprovingly. *if look's could kill* Spencer thought. "He's a top government scientist, slash scientific adviser. Fifty six years old. British born to Dutch parents. By all accounts he should have been home." "What would our killer want with a scientist." Summer wondered aloud. "No idea Spencer" responded. Maybe finding that out could be the key to solving this case. Or maybe its just a red herring. How long has she been cold" Spencer asked Summer completely ignoring Kay. "Anything between eight and ten hours."

"What about the cause of death."

"Victim died from a Brocken neck" Summer answered bluntly. "We also suspect that she was drained of her blood. Most likely after she was killed."

"Odd" Spencer mused aloud. "You sure if was after"

"Pretty sure" Kay answered this time. "Will know for deff when I get her on my table"

"I've seen enough" Spencer said as he turned and walked out of the room. Summer got to her feet and chased after him.

She hurried down downstairs and outside. Catching up with Spencer by a black BMW. "You know we are not chasing your normal murderer here. Don't you?" Spencer asked in hushed tone's.

"There's such a thing as a normal murderer now" Summer responded sarcastically.

"You know what I mean" Spencer said.

"Yeah, vampires. But that's just insane. They don't exist."

"If telling yourself that helps you sleep at night. But you have seen the evidence. Like Sherlock Holmes once said. If you eliminate the impossible. Then whatever is left no matter how improbable must be the truth."

"He wasn't real either" Summer forced a wry smile.

"Hey believe what you like. Vampire's are out there. You don't have to take my word for it"

"Should you really be admitting that" Summer taunted.

"Not really. But you had already worked it out. Even if you are trying to deny it."

"What's really going on here?" Summer demanded.

"A whole bunch of stuff that is considered above top secret"

"Let me guess. It's all on a need to know basis and I don't need to know"

"Your good" Spencer laughed. "I could tell you. But then I would have to kill you" He flashed a wicked smiled. The unwitting detective had no idea how true that statement was. "I can tell you this. Top brass are very concerned with a vamp called Lucius."

Lucius there was a name that rang a bell. But Summer couldn't remember why. Then it hit her, like a freight train. Lucius was the vampire from her last dream.

"You ok" Spencer asked, noticing Summer was lost in thought.

"Look I have to go. I'm sure you already know where to find me" Without another word Summer walked away and towards her car.

Harry Worthington sat in his office. He was in the middle of a budget meeting with his Health Secretary. When he felt the soft vibrations of his secret mobile phone, going off in his trouser pocket. Harry ignored the phone and listened to his Health Secretary, Alice Holiday. She was going over her plans to modernise the NHS. Making it more efficient and cost affective. At present the government was spending billions of tax payers money, just to keep the ailing NHS afloat.

Drastic changes were needed desperately and Alice was the woman to deliver them.

"If you thing these changes are what's needed to keep the NHS alive. Then I will support them one hundred percent." Harry ensured her.

"Thank you Prime Minister" Alice smiled. She was glad to have her bosses backing.

Harry watched as the pretty Health Secretary left his office. At thirty eight she had a great mind. Combined with good looks and bags of charisma. She was already very popular with the public. Many tipped her to be the next PM. But not just yet. Harry hoped. A few years in the future perhaps. If she avoided any major cock ups. The press could be very unforgiving these days. Cutting short many a political carer over the smallest of misdemeanours. *like bloody sharks.* He thought. *once they smell blood they go straight in for the kill.*

Harry fished his phone from his pocket and hit redial. The phone rang just three times before being answered. "Sir, it's Spencer"

"Where the hell have you been. I haven't heard from you in weeks!!." Harry Scolded. "I've been working Sir" Spencer replied coolly. "Tracking down the target has been difficult. Vampire's aren't exactly my area of expertise. I'm having to use alternative tactics."

"I don't care what you do. I just want results."

"I understand that Sir. But the reason I called is that you may have a bigger problem.

I have just left home of one Professor William Snyder. His wife has been found dead and Professor Snyder is no where to be seen. Even the police can't get hold of him." The line went silent for a few moments.

"Damn it" Harry Cursed. He's got him hasn't he"

"The Vampire Sir? That's unconfirmed"

"Don't unconfirmed me." Harry responded angrily. "Lucius has Snyder I have no doubt. If Snyder blabs The vampire will be coming for me next. You better get here pronto"

"I'm on my way." Spencer told his boss. Harry hung up the phone. He opened a slim metal case and took out a Cuban cigar. Now seemed as good as time as any to smoke it.

As promised Giles Price was still sitting at the table inside the café. Without so much of a greeting Summer pulled up a chair and sat herself down. "Ok she said I am all ear's"

Giles Price smiled. And looked at his watch. "Only four hours thought it may take you longer than that to come around."

Summer shot him a stern, don't mess with me look.

"Ok then straight to the facts. You come from a long line of Demon Hunters dating back over two millennia. Your green eyes and red hair are physical trademarks of a Hunter. But more importantly you have superior strength, speed, stamina and agility to that of a normal human being."

"Can't say I have noticed any of this" Summer said.

"I dare say you haven't your true potential has probably being lying dormant. But you are having the dreams. So I am guessing your powers will manifest them selves soon enough. To be honest we thought the Hunter line might be gone. There hasn't been a Demon Hunter since the eighteenth century. The last demon Hunter was a young woman called Sarah Richards.

"My surname" Summer interrupted.

"Precisely" Price continued. Sarah's family was found slaughtered at her home one evening. Her husband and son both dead. She also had a little girl. Who was found tied to a chair. When they cut her free, they realised she had been sired by a vampire. As for Sarah herself. Her body was never found. Rumour had it that she fled, out of grief and despair. She just couldn't bring herself to slay her own daughter. Even if she knew it wasn't really her anymore."

"I remember that" Summer cut in. "It was one of my dreams. I tasted her tears and felt her pain. The demon wore the face of her child. No matter how hard Sarah tried she couldn't bring herself to slay the child. But if the vampire killed her children how can I be a descendant."

"Maybe she remarried and had more children. Maybe fate chose a different line through the family. I'm not sure on that one I'm afraid. The Powers work in mysterious ways."

"Powers" Summer asked feeling ever more confused.

"They are who control our destiny. Mysterious God like beings that watch over us. In truth we know very little about them. But we know hey exist. Through magic's and visions."

"Visions!?"

"Like your dreams for instance."

"Maybe that's it" Summer said everything starting to click into place. "The vampire from my dream the one who Butchered Sarah's family. He has the same name as our current perpetrator. Lucius."

"Lucius of the Fall" Price said knowingly. A very old vampire. It was said he was one of the vampire Kings key lieutenants. Maybe he is why the Powers are intervening of late. They see the rise of a new vampire king."

"Why is that so important?" A bemused Summer asked. "And you haven't explained how you know all this"

"One question at a time. You see vampires are normally solitary creatures hunting and killing on their own sometimes in pairs. That's all they do stick to the shadows kill a few homeless people. Or sometimes when someone goes missing without a trace, that's usually a vampire. That's about as bad as it gets. But when a King comes along other vampires will converge around him. You see he has the power and authority to unite the vampires. To organise them into something more than just killers in the shadows. The last time a vampire king came to prominence they created the Knights Templar. Fooled a lot of people. They had a temple for their base, became very wealthy and damn well near conquered the known world."

"I see" Summer said sitting back. "A vampire King is very bad news. But so far Lucius just seems to be on a random killing spree. "

They won't be random. There will be method to them. Even if we can't see it yet. It may just be the smallest of thread's that ties them all together. But its there you just have to look in the right place."

"So again Mr Price I ask you. Who are you, how did you know how and where to find me?"

"Back in the day we called ourselves the guardian's of knowledge. As long as there as been a hunter there has been a guardian at their side. Our families have shared a mystical bond for hundreds of years. I used ancient magic's and er . . . google to track you down" Price gave a warm smile.

"So I guess my next question has to be, how do you kill a vampire"

"Well defeating a vampire is a case of separating fact from fiction. Lets start with what doesn't work. Holy water and crosses as far as I know has no affect. There just fairy tales. They can also cross water and they don't need an invite to enter some ones home. Although vampire's are allergic to bright sunlight. It doesn't kill them. But it certainly weakens and disorientates them. So they do prefer the night. A wooden or silver stake through the hart will kill them. Decapitation is also a very affective way to slay a vampire. Fire will also do the trick. As for modern weapons. As far as my information goes they are untested. Best not rely on Guns I would suggest.

Summer made a mental note of everything Price told her. The knowledge he gave might be the difference between living and dying. Summer had no doubt now, it was her destiny to fight Lucius. Her destiny to kill him. "How do you know all this information is correct"

"Good question" Price said. "Books and papers handed down my family from generation to generation. Vampires aren't the only thing out there by the way. But we haven't the time to go into all that. We must concentrate on Lucius. We need to find out his next target and fast."

"I should go back to the station. Maybe they have found something useful on the last victim. Something that might give us some kind of clue to what's going on."

"Good idea. Look here is my card. Call me any time. I am completely at your disposal."

"Don't worry. You will hear from me. All this vampire and demon stuff is scaring the crap out of me." Summer gave Giles a playful smile and walked out of the café.

Chapter eight

Lucius walked into a large office. Located in the old abandoned warehouse he was using as his base of operations. "How are we feeling Professor Snyder?" He asked the newly sired vamp.

"I feel great" The Professor answered. "I have truly been reborn."

"Tell me. How did you feel drinking from your dead wife?"

"I didn't feel anything to be honest. Which is strange considering she was my wife. But I felt noting for her at all. She just food."

"Good." Lucius smiled "Anyway I think my men have rounded up most of the things you require for your experiments."

The professor smiled and walked over to a table to check his equipment. They had brought him Microscopes, Petri dishes, test tubes. Syringes and beakers. There were also various chemicals that he wasn't sure would be of much use. "What did you do raid a school."

"Something like that" Lucius grinned. "I know it's basic but we can't go back to your lab. Its too risky. So your gonna have to make do."

"I'm sure I can manage. But there is no guarantee I can make this work on a vampire. Patient Zero was one in a million, when it came to humans. There's no telling what the effects could be. It could take me days, weeks even years to perfect a working formula."

"Lets see what we can do in days" Lucius pressed.

"What about Patient Zero" Snyder asked. "I can't conduct my experiments without her"

"Don't worry. I've got everything in hand" Lucius ensured the professor.

The Police were now at Downing Street and the whole place was on lock down. No could enter and no one could leave. Harry was now passing Spencer off as his personal body guard. Which thankfully no one seemed to question. But even with all these men. Harry was still concerned. It wasn't man they were protecting him against It was a vampire and goodness knows what he is capable of. Would the armed police really be a match against him. At least his family would be safe they had been escorted to his wife's mothers and were also under police protection just in case. Harry felt lonely going to bed that night. It wasn't often he slept on his own in this particular room. The bed felt cold and empty without his wife. At the time he needed her most they had to be apart.

If I get through this I will end things with Veronica Change myself for the better. Harry promised himself before trying to get some sleep. Harry tossed and turned for hours before finally falling asleep.

It was six in the morning and DCI Adam Greenhorn was in a panic. He had just being informed that Detective Kevin Moore. The man assigned to watch over Jenny Worthington and her children. Hadn't called in yet. If something had gone wrong his head was on the chopping block for sure. He waited impatiently for Summer to arrive at the station. He knew she would be at least another five minutes but he needed her here now. When Summer arrived at the station she was immediately greeted by her superior officer and ushered out. "We will take my car" Adam said urgently as they exited the Police station. Across the street Adams black range rover was parked and was ready and waiting. Engine running. As the approached the car Officer Vardy stepped out of the drivers seat. Adam jumped in as Summer sprinted round to the passenger side. Adam put the car into gear and sped off. Summer decided not to talk in the car. Best let Adam concentrate on his driving. He was trying to make a fifteen minute journey in five minutes. They got there in eight. Both Summer and Adam hurriedly got out of the car and ran over to a black Vauxhall Astra. Summer could see Kevin's body Slumped inside his head resting on the steering Wheel. She opened the drivers door and pushed Kevin's body so he was upright on the seat. "Jesus!"

Summer exclaimed in shock. The mans throat had been cut and he was covered in blood.

"He bled to death" Summer told her boss. "Sick bastard slit his throat. Didn't even drink him"

"Never mind that for now" Adam replied. "Front door is open. Follow me." The DCI took point as the two detectives walked inside the Harrison house. The home of the Prime Minister's In-laws. It was a modest house. The interior was everything you would expect from a working class home.

"Clear" Adam said as he walked into the Kitchen. "Nothing down here. Lets try upstairs"

They crept up the stairs gun's at the ready. Just in case. Adam held out his gun and kicked open the bedroom door. There was blood everywhere in the master bedroom. The walls and the floors were caked in the stuff. It looked like an abattoir. "This is a massacre" Adam said shaking his head in disgust. Stay there Summer you don't want to see this, trust me." As Adam took another couple of steps into the room trying his best to avoid the blood. He could see the bodies of an elderly couple. Or at least what was left of them. Limbs had been ripped off and guts had been pulled out, then strewn across the floor. *The sick bastard.* Adam thought as he backed out of the room. "That's What's left of Mr and Mrs Harrison. Lets check the other rooms for Mrs Worthington and the Kids" After what he had just seen. Adam had lost all hope of finding anyone alive. He kicked another door open. There was Clara and Jenny Worthington. Their dead bodies placed into a pose. As if they where a work of art of some kind. Jenny Worthington was sat up on a small wooden chair with her hand placed on Clara's head as she lay on the bed. Postured by the killer to look as if she was sleeping. Adam checked their pulses as a matter of formality. He was already pretty certain they were dead. "There gone" he shook his head. "Where's Amber" Summer asked.

"Damn it" Adam cursed. With all the blood and carnage he had failed to notice the youngest girl was missing. "Maybe she is in another room?" he said clutching at straws.

"There's two more rooms to check." Summer agreed.

Summer and Adam went about checking the last two rooms. But it proved to be fruitless. The bathroom was empty. It was the same story in the last bedroom. There was no indication anyone had been in there at all. There was no sign of the little girl anywhere.

Harry Worthington was woken by Chief Superintendent Brian Gold. Who had come straight to Downing Street with urgent news. "Sorry to wake you Sir. But I have bad news." Gold said mournfully. Harry could tell by the mans tone that he should prepare himself for the worst.

"I'm afraid Jenny and Clara have been found dead. Along with Jenny's parents. As for Amber we can't find her anywhere. I'm so sorry." The Chief Superintendent took a step back and turned away. Harry couldn't hold back his emotion. Tears streamed down his face like salt water waterfalls. His family butchered by a vampire and it was all his fault. "Ambers still alive then" Harry asked more in hope than anything else

"At this point we have no idea Sir. But we suspect she may have been taken hostage. So in all likely hood she is still alive."

"You have to find her" Harry Pleaded.

"You have to understand that we are dealing with a crazed psychopath here. There's no telling what demands he will make, Or what he may do if those demands are not met."

"I don't care what his demands are Chief Superintendent" Harry yelled through the tears. "Just get my little girl back."

"We will do everything we can Sir" Gold promised as he left the room. Seconds after Chief inspector Gold had left the room and had disappeared down stairs a call came through on Harry's smart phone. As he picked up the phone the display read Amber calling. Harry answered in a heart beat. "Amber?"

"Not Amber" came a menacing reply "Who are you?" Harry screamed "Where's Amber?"

"I think you know exactly who I am" Lucius said "As for Amber she is right here and alive. For now. Do you want to speak to your daddy" The vampire asked Amber as Harry listened. The next words he heard were those of his daughter. "Daddy I'm scared" Came her little voice. "I know sweetheart. I won't let him hurt you I promise. Daddy will save you." "I love you Dad . . . ." The phone was taken off her before she could finish her sentence.

"If you ever want to see your daughter again. Your going to do a little something for me. Understood."

"Yes, yes anything just don't hurt my little girl." Harry pleaded. The vampire proceeded to give Harry his instructions.

Summer had called Price on her Smartphone and had arranged to meet him at his hotel. Turned out Price was staying at a top end five star hotel. The man like to live in style. The entrance to the hotel even had doormen, who greeted her as she walked in. The hall of the hotel was as grand as she had ever seen. A spotless tiled floor. That was either faux marble or actual marble. Summer couldn't tell. Large and expensive works of art hung on the walls and a neat red carpet ran up the huge stairs. Summer walked up the impressive front desk and asked the clerk for Giles Price's room number. "My name is Summer Richards" She told the man. "He should be expecting me"

"Do you have any form of identification." Came the clerks snobbish reply.

"I think this should do" Summer said as she flashed her Police badge. The clerk suddenly became far more co-operative. Once inside Price's hotel room. Which was just as grand as the rest of the hotel. Summer explained recent event's. The death of Harry Worthington's family and the possible kidnapping of his youngest daughter.

"I've got to find her. I can't let anyone else die. I just can't."

"I know" Price replied reassuring her. "I can help you find her."

"How?" Summer asked desperate to know.

"I can cast a locater spell. I did one to find you. Although it didn't turn out exactly right. But I think I know where I went wrong."

"So there's magic now!?" An exasperated Summer asked. "What are you some sort of Warlock"

"No. not at all. I have certain knowledge and texts that allows me to cast the odd spell or too. And yes there has always been magic. It's just rarely used in this day and age. Science kind of took over. Look I hate to be abrupt but we haven't got time for this. I need a map of the city."

"I'll get one from the lobby" Summer said as she got off her chair. Moments later she returned to the room with a large fold out map. "Will this do"

"It will do just fine" Price smiled as he carefully unfolded the map and laid it out on the floor. He then opened his black brief case and pulled out several items. Including six candles a box of matches. Some bags of various herbs and spices. He selected a brownish looking herb and put the rest away. He then positioned the candles around the outside of the map. After he lit each candle individually. Price opened the bag containing the brown herb. He emptied the contents into his free hand and began chanting words in a foreign language. Most likely Latin summer guessed. Price then threw the brownish herb into the air and watched as it landed on the map. The herb seemed to land in random places. But a large clump did settle in one particular spot.

"Is that where we need to go." Summer asked pointing at the clump of herbs.

"Yes. that's were Lucius and the girl will be. The Spell detects and locates strong surges of supernatural energy."

"As in a powerful vampire." Summer added. "I know that area of town. There's an abandoned warehouse down there. I will go and check it out."

"Your not ready" Price warned. "You need the right weapons and training before you can go rushing in on a gang of vampires"

"I get that but by then it could be too late. I will go check it out strictly recon."

"You have a point. But be careful and don't engage unless you have no alternative."

Bearing his advice in mind Summer left the hotel and made her way to the Warehouse.

An hour later Summer was at the warehouse. The place was once used a storage facility for a once major high street chain. But that company had long since folded during the recession and the warehouse had been abandoned. The place was all boarded up and hadn't seen any legal use for years now. Summer made her way towards the warehouse. When a black BMW pulled up beside her. Spencer climbed out of the car to Summers dismay.

"We've been watching you. It's a MI5 thing. Do you want my help or not" Spencer asked knowing that the detective had little choice but to accept his offer.

"I will take any help I can get right now." Summer said begrudgingly. *Is MI5 following my every move now?* She wondered

"Then what are we waiting for. Lets find away in" Summer and Spencer walked around the perimeters of the old warehouse looking for a way to get inside. "Here" Spencer said as he noticed a side door that wasn't completely shut. Standing against the wall he pushed it open and peered around. "Clear" he whispered.

Summer followed Spencer inside a pocket size torch in her hand.

"Be careful with that" Spencer warned "We don't want to draw undue attention to ourselves."

"I know. But we also need to see where we are going. It's low light don't worry. We will use it sparingly."

They walked through the cold an dark warehouse. The building was completely silent. Not even the scuttle of rodents could be heard. "This place is too quiet. I don't like it" Summer spoke in hushed whispers.

They scoured the whole first floor and came up with nothing. "It's empty" Spencer spoke at last. "There's nothing here. Not even rats"

"And that's what worry's me. What have rats got to be scared of in an abandoned building like this?"

"Lets check the offices upstairs" They made their way towards the metal stair case that led up to the second floor. But before they could ascend four figures jumped down. Landing either side of the pair. Four bright yellow eyes glared at them through the darkness. They were surrounded by vampire's.

"It's a bloody trap" Spencer shouted as he fired bullets in the direction of an on coming vampire. Summer followed suit. The bullets where met by hisses of pain but little else. The vampires carried on advancing. "What do we do now" Spencer asked clearly getting scared.

"RUN!" Summer shouted. As Summer turned to run she felt the cold hand of a vampire grab her shoulder. Amazingly she was able to shake him off. *Might as well go down fighting.* She thought as turned round and landed a hard punch on a vampires face. The power of the blow forced the vampire to stagger back. Summer could see a look of surprise on the demon's face. The obviously weren't expecting an even fight. A vampire tried to ambush Summer from behind. But some how she sensed it coming. Spinning round quickly she grabbed the vampires arm. Using his own momentum she sent the demon crashing into another vampire. Causing them both to tumble to the floor. In survival mode now Summer sprinted to the exit without another thought.

As Summer made it outside into the daylight she could see Spencer's black BMW was still parked outside. The Spook hadn't made it out. But Spencer was a professional. She couldn't worry about him.

Her objective remained the same. She had to find Amber Worthington. But Price was right. Next time we would be packing more appropriate weaponry

Back in the warehouse Spencer was being carried up the metal stairs. Slung over the shoulder of a hulking vampire. They had quickly overpowered him as Summer made her escape. But he couldn't hold that against her. He would have done exactly the same if the roles had been reversed. The vampire took him into a small looking office. Where Spencer's captor unceremoniously dropped him onto the floor. Spencer moaned in pain as landed hard on his shoulder.

"Wasn't there two of them, Where's the girl?" Came an angry voice.

"She got away"

"How?" the lead vampire asked.

"She was strong. She was able to fight us off"

"Interesting" Lucius mused aloud. "No normal human is strong enough to be a match for us. She must be a Demon Hunter"

"A what" one of the vampires asked?

"I'm not going to explain" Lucuis Sneered. "Demon Hunter its pretty self explanatory."

Spencer lifted his head and tried to see what was going around him. There were five vampires in the room now. A taller vamp in a black suit and red tie, looked to be the on in charge. His movement caught the eye of the lead vampire. Lucius smiled and walked over. "It's you lucky day my friend" He hissed. "Today we are recruiting."

Lucius grabbed Spencer by the collar of his shirt and pulled him up to his feet.

Spencer refrained fro screaming as she saw the demons fangs. Lucius pushed Spencer's head to the side and sank his teeth into his neck. Spencer wanted to struggle free. But he couldn't it was if he was paralysed. His mind said move but his body wasn't responding. It wasn't long before Spencer felt himself fading. A weakness and tiredness began to take over. His eyelids became heavy. He wanted to keep his eyes open, knowing if he shut them he would be lost to the darkness forever. But it was over. Perhaps he shouldn't fight it. But then the vampire stopped drinking and let him go. Spencer had just enough energy to watch the vampire cut his own arm. "Drink" The monster told Spencer as he placed his bleeding arm in front of him. Spencer didn't need to be told twice he clutched the vampires arm and drank. He drank the vampires blood until he drifted into darkness. A darkness that offered him eternal damnation.

Harry Worthington sat in front of TV cameras waiting for his live press conference to start. He had no notes or script. But they weren't needed Lucius had made it clear what he had to say. Harry just hoped it would be enough to see the safe return of his daughter. A pretty young woman in a tiny skirt walked over to Harry with a make up tray and brush "Just need to touch up your makeup Sir" She told him as she started applying foundation with the small makeup brush. "There that should do you" She smiled before stepping out of the way.

"Ok everybody" came a yell from the young director. "We are on in five, four, three . . . . two . . . . one. We are live!"

There was a slight hesitation by Harry as he composed himself, before he started talking. "Ladies and Gentleman" Harry started in a grave tone. "I have important news for you today. As you may have heard already this morning. My Parent In-laws, my wife and eldest daughter where found murdered. My youngest daughter Amber is missing presumed kidnapped. As you will realise this has been a most upsetting and distressing time for me. But non the less you deserve to know the truth. Now I understand what I am about to tell you will seem strange at first. You may not want to believe it. But I assure you for once everything I say will be the truth. The perpetrator of my families murder is not a man but a vampire. Yes you heard me correctly. I said Vampire. These monsters or demons if you like. Have lived amongst us for years. And those of us in government have always known. It was decided many decades ago that the general public should be protected from this information. A decision made by governments world wide I should add. These decisions were made with your best interests at heart. We wanted to avoid a mass hysteria. We didn't people too scared to go out at night. Or even worse try and become vigilante vampire slayers.

But the revaluations don't end there. In the past five years under my leadership. We have been rounding up these vampires and conducting various experiments on them. Experiments that would be illegal if carried out on a human being. I apologise for these lies and for my sin's. Obviously I will resign from government with immediate affect. Leaving Deputy Prime Minister Charles Thomas in charge. I hope you the general public can find it in your hearts to forgive me. Thank you and goodbye" People in the studio were dumb founded at what they had just heard. Recent events had obviously driven the poor Prime Minister to madness.

PART THREE

The Sins of Our father's

Chapter nine

Langley, Virginia
CIA Headquarters.

News of the British Prime minister was reaching all corners of the western world. People were already speculating on internet forums. To whether there was any truth in Harry Worthington's ramblings. So far it was noting to worry about. Just the usual conspiracy theorists. Most people were putting it down to a psychotic episode. The loss of the Prime ministers family driving him over the edge. Making up monsters in his head to explain his past mistakes. But CIA Agent Raphael Monroe, new it wouldn't be long before people with "proof" stepped forward. That was something the CIA couldn't risk happening.

Monroe sprinted down the hall towards his bosses office. He needed to talk to Deputy Director Logan Reece immediately. He burst through the door and into the Deputy Director's Secretary's office. Lilah West gave the intruder a harsh stare. She was a thin lipped women with a sour face. Long stringy back hair that had obviously been died far too much. But she was immaculately dressed and kept a very tidy and organised desk. Deputy Director Reece often said he couldn't get by without her. "He's in a meeting with Reade from accounting."

"This early in the morning?" The Secretary just continued her glare. "Look this is very important. If I thought it could wait I wouldn't of ran down here." Still without saying a word to Raphael. Lilah sighed and pressed a button on her intercom. "Sorry to disturb you Mr Reece but I have agent Monroe here for you. He says it's urgent." "Ok Give me a minute" Came the gruff tones of the Deputy Director. Moments later agent Jonas Reade head of internal accounting walked out of Logan Reece's office. Quickly followed by the Deputy Director himself. "This better be good Monroe" Reece growled as he motioned the agent into his office. The tall, balding Deputy Director sat behind his desk and patiently waited for Monroe to talk. "You will be better off seeing this for yourself Sir" Raphael advised. "If click onto the BBC live news feed right now. You will see what I mean."

Logan Reece clicked on his mouse and watched his computer screen. "God damn" Logan Reece cursed as he finished watching the video. "What does that limey bastard think he's doing."

"Tell me about it Sir this could open a huge can of worms."

"Worms" Reece yelled "This could open Pandora's box. If they find out the British Prime Minister has been working with the CIA. The proverbial will hit the fan. "What the hell is going on there."

"According to my information. There was an incident at the British experimental facility. Several vampires and demons managed to escape. A vampire known as Lucius decided to go on a revenge fuelled killing spree. Culminating in the homicide of Harry Worthington's family. Chatter is that's what tipped our man over the edge."

"I'm going to need you on the next plan to London. Once there you can Liaise with our UK agent Jody Simm. I want you to organise a clean up operation. Send in a team to infiltrate the facility. Recover whatever data and samples you can. Then burn the lab to the ground. As for Harry Worthington. Take whatever action necessary to silence him. Am I understood?"

"Perfectly Sir" Monroe replied. Raphael went back to his office and onto his laptop. A few clicks later he had managed to secure last minute tickets on a flight to Heathrow. He then opened up his email account and sent a message to Jody Simm. Instructing her to meet him at the airport. Two hours later Agent Raphael Monroe was at Washington National Airport.

London England

Back in the hotel room. Summer sat on a comfy red arm chair as she explained the events at the warehouse. To Giles Price. "Lucius has the girl there

I am sure of it" She told him. I'll have t get tooled up properly. With stakes and swords and go in again."

"I feel I need to remind you that killing Lucius is your main priority. I know that may sound harsh. But if he see's the girl as your weakness. Then he won't hesitate to use her against you. You will have to learn to control you emotions."

"I see your point, I really do. But I am not going to let anyone else die" Summer said defiantly. "Can you procure the weapons I need.?"

That shouldn't be a problem. But having the weapons wont be enough. You have to know how to use them. Going into battle with a weapon you can't use is just as dangerous as going in empty handed."

"Then teach me. Isn't that what you are here for?"

"Well yes" Price admitted. "I suppose I can give you a crash course once we have a sword. But after that we may need to consider full time training."

"You mean quit my job. I'm not sure I can do that"

"Well its up to you" Price told her. "I can't force you to do anything. I can only advise."

Harry Worthing had been let into his former office one last time to clear out is belongings. Two Police Officers waited out side in the hall. Once he had collected his stuff he was going to be escorted to the Police station to be questioned. They were very keen to question him. About what he said in his press conference. If he had been anyone else he would have been arrested already. Lawyers and government officials had already been on TV trying to disregard everything Harry had said. Trying to convince the media the former Prime Minister had a moment of madness. Due to the intense pressure he was under and the shock of recent events. It was a convincing argument that seemed to be working. Of course there will always be diehard's who want to believe. Harry took his secret mobile phone from his desk. He prised it open and took out his sim card. Reaching under his desk he took out his single malt scotch and glass. He poured himself a large shot, placed the sim card in his mouth and washed it down with a big gulp of scotch. He didn't want anyone finding the numbers on his sim card. The country and himself could be in big trouble. If they knew he had been colluding with the CIA. Once he was ready the police ushered him out the back to a waiting car. They wanted to keep his visit to the station as low profile as possible.

It had been a long flight from Washington to London. Sat right behind a screaming child that wouldn't shut up. Raphael Monroe was tired and jet lagged. But he had important work to do. A large clean up operation to organize. He entered the lengthy cue at border control and waited to be processed and let into the country. No problems at border control. The uniformed man looked over his passport, stamped it and let him through. Agent Monroe then went straight to the luggage carousel and waited for what seemed like an eternity for his case to come round. Raphael collected his small black suit case and left the terminal to find Jody Simm.

The female agent waited patiently, for her fellow American to come through the terminal. The Asian American had heard that Raphael Monroe was quite a catch and from the photo she had received she had to agree. The thirty four year old agent had think black hair, that rolled into tight curls. He had dark olive skin and deep penetrating brown eyes. A baby sitting mission she was more than looking forward to. She had already booked a hotel room for the visiting agent, four star's on CIA expenses. As Jody clocked agent Monroe walking towards her she realised he was even better looking in the flesh. In his tight blue jeans white shirt and black leather jacket. He walked straight over to her an introduced himself with a smile that could charm a nun. Jody told Monroe that his hotel was sorted and asked if he needed any rest. "I do" Monroe admitted. "But we need to get cracking. We can risk things escalating"

"Agreed" Smiled the pretty Asian American.

Boy was she pretty Monroe thought. She had an amazing body for a thirty eight year old. And she wore cloths that showed it off. Tight business suit blazer that hugged her in all the right places and a short pencil skirt. She wore her long glossy black hair down and it framed her pretty face perfectly. "I've got four of my best men on stand by" Jody told Him in her thick New York accent.

"Good" Monroe said. Lets get to your office and get started. The sooner I can get back home. To American soil the better."

Giles Price had managed to procure a silver edged katana from a small antique shop down town. It was in good condition and most importantly still razor sharp. It had cost him five hundred pounds, small change to a wealthy man like himself. Fortunately for Price his ancestors had the foresight to stow away vast sums of money. That was either paid to them or recovered from various demons. The money was eventually used to set u one of the worlds first banks. Even more fortunate one that had so far avoided the pit falls of the recession. Although the bank itself was run by more business minded people. Price was still major share holder. Those shares were enough to allow him to live quite comfortably. He handed the sword to Summer. She slid it out of it's scabbard and looked closely at the blade. I was so well polished she could see her reflection in the cold hard steal. As she swung the katana in the air Price could see that she was meant to wield it. The grace and accuracy in which she moved was startling for a novice. "Impressive" Price admitted "You were truly born for this" He smiled brightly like a child at a candy store. "But we still have to make sure you are ready for battle."

"I guess we will find out soon enough"

"Sooner than you think" Price cautioned as he walked out of the room. Moments later he walked back in. holding a katana of his own. "I bought a spare" He smiled.

"What was it two for one" Summer laughed.

"En guard" Price called as he positioned himself in to fighting stance. Sword pointing towards Summer. The Detective duly obliged. Summer brought her sword down. But Price intercepted the blow. "Don't hold back" He told her. He fainted left luring Summer in. She fell for it. "That would of been your right kidney" You have to read your opponent. Don't let him lure you in. Again." Summer tried to take Price surprise but he parried the blow. "Good. I like he told her" Your enemies won't wait for you. So why wait for them. Now your learning." Using her superior strength and speed Sumer brought her Sword round hard and fast. Price met the blow with his katana but the force of the blow knocked him off balance. Summer took advantage and swept the Guardian off his feet. Price fell on his backside. Keen to take advantage Summer went in the killer blow. But Price dodged out of the way. Summer felt something sharp pressed against her stomach. She looked down to see Giles Price holding at dagger against her. "A concealed blade can be a lethal weapon" He warned. "Never let your guard down. Even if you think your opponent is defeated. Lucius is old and cunning. He will have many tricks up his sleeve. Now put this on." Price instructed as he pulled a piece of black material out of his pocket.

"A blind fold!? How can I fight if I can't see?"

"Through sound and instinct. You enemies are at home in he dark. Demons can see as well in the dark as you can in the day. You can't afford that to be a disadvantage. You must embrace the darkness like they have. Become one with it. Let it shape you. Or are already defeated."

"I see your point" Summer conceded as she tied the blindfold on tightly. Price went in for a surprise attack. Summer span round and parried the blow.

"Good" Price acknowledged. From now on this is how we train."

Chapter ten
CAI headquarters UK

The operatives were almost ready. Four highly trained ex navy seals. The best of the best. Agent Raphael Monroe just wanted to go through the finale checks. "Stakes Wooden and Silver?" He asked.

"Check" Alpha team leader responded.

"Automatic riffles loaded with silver bullets"

"Check"

"C4 explosives and detonator"

"Check"

"Good everything is ready. "Lets make sure your helmet cam is working." Monroe tapped a few buttons on his laptop. "Ok turn and face agent Simm. Give me a wave agent." Monroe watched Jody's movements on the infra red camera. "Good. Ok so I can see what you see. I will run point from here. You understand the mission?"

"Yes Sir" Alpha leader responded "Collect the sample and kill everything that moves. Plant the explosives and blow the place off the map."

"That's right. I want you in and out as fast as humanly possible. Go, go, go."

The four men marched out of the office.

"So agent Simm I think we have a good half an hour or so to waste before they reach the target." Agent Jody Simm smiled and hitched up her skirt. Monroe walked over and kissed her hard and passionately sliding his hand down her silk knickers. Twenty five minutes later they were interrupted by Alpha leader. "Sir" Came a voice over the com's.

"Damn Monroe cursed as he pulled himself of agent Simm and pulled his trousers back up. "

Sir" are you there.

"I'm here Alpha leader. Go head.

"We have made it to the facilities elevator."

"Ok good" Monroe said "Now on the wall there should be a retinal scanner. They use to activate the elevator. You will need to remove that. carefully and then hit the override code on the panel beneath. Simm and Monroe watched the live feed from Alpha leader's camera. As one of the men used some sort of crowbar, to prise the retinal scanner off the wall. "Can you see the control panel?" Monroe asked

"Yes Sir. We are ready for the cod.

"Ok the sequence is. Charlie . . . . Echo . . . . five . . . zero . . . . Romeo . . . . zero.

"Copy. It worked elevator is active"

So far good. All the information the Deputy Director had given Monroe was panning out perfectly.

"We are in the base. Making our way to the main lab now. "Sir there are still White coats down here." White Coats was a code the special ops team used for scientists.

"I know Alpha leader. Remember anything that moves?" Monroe told him coldly

"Sir!" Alpha leader responded in compliance.

The com went silent. The two agents watched the feed on the laptop. As scientists ran for cover. The men opened fire. It was like something out of a horror movie. The bodies of scientists fell and slumped to the floor as they were hit by multiple bullets. It was a blood bath. Simm had to turn away. She could stomach any more. Monroe kept his eyes glued to the screen. He had to be responsible for the teams every move.

If something went wrong and he missed it. Well it wasn't worth thinking about.

"They really are covering their track's over this" she said coldly

"I know. Spend millions on a project and the millions more to cover it up. No wonder we are in recession. But that's people at the top for you. Throw money at everything. Unless its our wages.

"I know" Simm agreed. With a smile.

"Sir" Alpha leader's voice came over the com again. The sample its not here."

"What do you mean it's got to be there. What were those coats working on?"

"No idea Sir But the sample you want. It's not here."

"God Damn it. Snyder must of kept it somewhere else."

"Ok plant the C4 and get out of there."

The com went quiet once more. Monroe watched as the teams explosive expert carefully set the C4. On the labs structural weak points.

"The explosives are planted" Alpha leader informed over the com's a few mintutes later. "we are evac right now"

"Good contact me when your out" Monroe turned to agent Jody Simm. The sexual chemistry was still bubbling between the two. They couldn't wait to finish what they started. But Raphael gave Jody a look that said this would have to wait a while longer yet. The mission had to come first.

The call came in ten minutes later followed by a loud explosion. Alpha leaders on-helmet camera picked up a cloud of dust and debris rising from the underground lab. It had been a job well done. But as the operatives made there way to their vehicle events took a terrible turn.

"I think I've just seen something" Alpha leader said. "There it is again something moving in the shadows"

"Think I glimpsed it too" Monroe confirmed as he saw some sort of movement in the back ground. I couldn't see a heat signature on the infra cam. It could be a vamp. Id get out of there now" Monroe ordered. But he was too late. Something came up close on the camera. There was a loud scream and the live feed went black. Monroe was left with no visual. But he still had sound. He could hear the blood curdling screams of the operatives. As whatever else was out there. Killed Monroe's men. An eerie silence followed. The men were dead. "Shit!" Agent Monroe cursed loudly.

"Those poor men" Jody Simm's voice cracked. Those screams told her enough about they way they died. It couldn't of been pleasant.

Training had been harder than Summer could of imagined. Especially the parts when she was blindfolded. But she knew it was necessary. Even if this was just crash course for the time being. But after all the hard training. Worked still beckoned. There was still case to be solved. Harry Worthington and been brought in for questioning. His belonging had been confiscated and his office searched. Adam and Summer had been authorised to conduct the interrogation. The had left Harry to stew for a good few hours in the cold dank holding cell. Before transferring him to the interview room. The detectives entered the room together, Styrofoam coffee cups in hand. They both pulled up a seat opposite former Prime Minister. Adam Checked his watch before clicking on the tape recorder. "Interview commenced at fourteen hundred hours." He stated for the benefit of the recording. "Ok Harry" Adam started. "Lets not beat around the bush. Amongst your belongings we found an old mobile phone. Obviously we have checked this phone. We found that the sim card had been removed. But our tech team were able to pull certain information from the phones circuit board. I bet you didn't know we could do that" Adam smiled. "From the that we discovered that no text messages had been sent or received. The mobile had been used for calls only.

Looks like you covered your tracks well. We found that very few calls had been made. And that they had been made to only four different numbers. Our tech team have been able to find out who some of these numbers belonged to. Shall I continue."

Harry just sat in silence and nodded his head.

"Two of your contacts were obviously very careful. We couldn't find any known identities under those numbers. But one number belonged to a Veronica White. Who we assume is your mistress. Or a contact of a sexual nature."

Harry nodded in agreement.

The other number is the one we are interested in. A number belonging to a phone, owned by Professor William Snyder. What was your relationship with William Snyder" Adam Probed

"He was the lead scientist in the experiments we conducted"

"The experiments on the vampires" Summer asked

Harry nodded his head.

"For the benefit of the tape, Harry is nodding his head" Adam said.

"Why did you do this?" Summer wanted to know

It started when Amber. My little girl was diagnosed with Leukaemia. Do you either of you have children?" Adam nodded. "Well can you imagine what its like to be told your child may have as little as two years to live. We tried everything. Even bone a marrow transplant did little to halt the dieses. Then one desperate night Some one informed me about a program the Russians were supposedly working on in secret. Rumours had it that they were trying to use vampire blood to cure illness and to create the perfect super soldier. But they had never made any significant headway. Or so we are led to believe. Of course official word is that no such experiments ever took place. So five years ago we started our own program. We set up a lab underground and started hunting and capturing vampire's." *Amongst other creatures of a supernatural origin.* But Harry wasn't about to go into that. The Detectives were having enough trouble coming to terms with the existence of vampires. No use telling them that was just the tip of the iceberg. "Eventually we where able to find a cure. But it had unforeseen side effects."

Like What exactly?" Adam asked.

"Not a sudden thirst for blood if that's what you think. It heightened her IQ, improved her stamina and poise, possibly her strength too. But I wasn't going to subject her to anymore tests. We just monitored the situation so to speak.

"In what way" Summer as keen to know.

"Just kept a keen eye on her in Dance class and Physical education. She started to outperform all the other children. So obviously we new there could be money to be made. If we could develop a serum that could enhance a humans abilities. God knows this county needs extra funds."

"So this is how you justify everything is it" Adam reacted angrily. "Your ill daughter and the state of the countries finances."

"No. nothing justifies what I did. I am just giving you the facts."

"How did you cure Amber in the end?" Summer pressed further." "

I don't know" Harry lied. "I didn't really understand it. Only William Snyder knew" "Do you think that's what the vampires took Professor Snyder an Amber. They want to continue the experiments for the selves. Develop a serum to make them even stronger."

"Oh God. You don't think?" Harry couldn't finish the sentence But all three of them knew what was on his mind. The idea of vampires experimenting on Amber. Didn't bare thinking about.

"What aren't you telling us Harry. You couldn't of set this up on your own. Who was helping you."

"There was no outside help. If that's what you mean"

"Stop lying Harry" Adam demanded. We found a Swiss bank account. Under the name Harry Harrison. Harrison is your wife's maiden name. The bank account has seen large transfers of money from America in the last five years. We can't trace were the money has come from. Because we keep hitting hit firewalls. Firewall's only someone like the CIA would have. Are you working with the CIA Harry?"

"I'm not working with CIA. Even if I was. They would deny all knowledge. You wouldn't be able to touch them. You must know that."

"Is that some kind of warning" Summer asked.

"No" Harry responded "I am just stating that it would be a waste of your time pursing it. Look detectives just find my daughter and bring her back to me. Alive. Then I will tell you everything." No lies no more holding back. But find my little girl."

Adam turned and looked at Summer. She nodded in agreement to what Adam was thinking. Both detective's knew they had no choice. They had no leverage over Harry and not enough evidence to hold Harry in custody. Harry wasn't going to divulge any more information until his daughter was safe.

"Interview concluded at fourteen twenty." Adam said as he switched of the recorder. "We have an idea where she might be." "Then why haven't you got her then!" Harry roared disapprovingly.

"You know it's not as simple as that Sir. If the kidnapper see's cops swarming the place he will probably panic and . . . ." Adam stopped short of saying kill her.

"Do something stupid" He told Harry instead. I sent my top agent DI Summer Richards on recon. To where we think the vampire is hold up. Quite frankly she was lucky to come back alive. An operative we now know was working for you wasn't so lucky. Spencer Smith. Although we suspect that's a pseudonym. His involvement is not important for now"

"Look we will do all we can" Summer tried to ensure Harry. We don't want any harm to come to Amber either. There has been enough death already."

"I know you will" Harry said softly. But he was beginning to loose any hope that his daughter would be found alive.

Amber Worthington was in a fragile state. In nothing but underwear and a operating gown she was strapped to a cold metal table. She almost wished she had died with her family. There screams for help etched in her conscious. Probably for ever. At first Amber wondered why they had spared her. But the reason why soon became clear.

They wanted her blood. The vampires must know how the cure had enhanced certain abilities. The obviously wanted it for themselves. With no daylight or clocks Amber had no idea how long she had been prisoner. It felt like weeks. But could easily be just days. But the vampires had taken several blood samples. The demons weren't exactly delicate. Often struggling to find the vein they were looking for. When she wasn't strapped to the table Amber was thrown into a small office. Where she was only given water, beard and porridge for food. They only fed her because they needed her alive for there experiments. Amber she was in a living nightmare. If there was a hell Amber then this was it.

As Professor Willaim Snyder had suspected. Amber Worthington's blood was the key. Although it had been Lycan blood. A kind of werewolf. That had proved crucial in finding Ambers cure. It had proved to be the least tainted blood. Containing more human DNA than other demon's they had tested. But it was the way Amber's genetic code had accepted and merged with Lycan DNA. That had surprised Snyder. Their genes merged, married and mutated. Creating something new, something stronger. Harry had forbade more tests on his little girl. But now there was nothing to stop him. He was determined to find out what made the girl so special. Back in the lab Lucius had overheard talking about the surprising results regarding Ambers cure. Now he was demanding a similar formula for himself. Lucus hopped to create a superior race of vampires. Stronger, faster and remove their allergy to sunlight. If they achieved this Lucius believed they would be unstoppable.

As he studied a sample of Ambers blood. Snyder could see that it had stabilised for now. There been no more changes no new mutations. There was no telling what kind of reaction if any the serum would have on a vampire. The was only one sure way to find out. It wasn't too difficult to create a similar formula he had used on Amber. All the hard work had been done years ago in the lab.

Lucius was interrupted in his thoughts by Professor Snyder. "I thought you may want to know that I think I may be on to something. By singling out certain genes in patient Zero's blood and combining it wit . . . ."

Lucius cut Snyder off mid sentence. "Spare me the techno babble. Will it work"

"We won't know until we test it. In a combat situation preferably."

Shouldn't be difficult to arrange. I have a small problem that needed taking care of and plenty of willing volunteers. Recently Lucius had sired several vampires. All were men highly trained in combat and espionage. They worked special ops for their governments. The men had included former SAS and navy Seals. The best thing was that no one would come looking for these men. They would be written off as collateral damage and forgotten about. And people say vampires are monsters. "Spencer" Lucius hissed. "I have a job for you. First I want you to go with the professor. He will administer an injection. That should make you stronger. You may need to give it an hour or two to kick in. When you think your ready I want you to seek out that detective Summer Richards. She is strong and powerful and could be become a problem. It would be prudent to eliminate her before she is able to tap into her full potential."

Harry Worthington had been released from custody for the time being. There would be no further questioning until Amber was saved. He want back to number ten downing street. Even though he was no longer Prime Minister and would be resigning from government. This was still his home for another two or three days. On the TV. The news channel were calling it a two horse race to be next Prime Minister. It was between Deputy PM Charles Thomas or the pretty young health secretary. Alice Holiday. Who was being hotly tipped to be the second ever female PM. Harry's phone rang he fished it out of his trouser pocket. It was an unknown number but Harry answered it anyway. "You've done well Harry." Came an obscured voice. "As promised your daughter will be returned to you. She will be waiting for you downtown at the pizza place. She will be wearing a red hoody." The phone went dead. Harry didn't hesitate he didn't even think. He grabbed his coat and left the house.

Twenty minutes later he found the pizza place the vampire had spoke of. As Harry walked inside. He could see all the people in the restaurant staring at him. There's that crazy Prime Minister. They where probably thinking and saying to one another. But Harry didn't care he just wanted to see his daughter. *Was that her. It had to be.* Harry thought as he saw a little girl in a red top. Hood pulled over her head. Obscuring her face. She was sitting with a pretty young lady. The pretty lady made swift eye contacted with Harry got to her feet and left the table. She walked passed Harry without even looking at him. It was like she hadn't even seen him. Harry raced over to the table and sat down. "Amber, honey is that" "Daddy" Came a terrified little voice. "It's ok honey" Harry comforted as he gave his only daughter a big hug. "Everything is going to be ok" Harry removed the hood and looked at the little girls face. This wasn't Amber what the hell was going on here. Harry stepped back in shock. As the little girl ran over to the young lady. The young lady smiled at him and then walked off with the young girl. *What was she looking at?* Suddenly he saw it there was a red dot on his chest. The red dot suddenly moved upwards. Before Harry Worthington had time to process another thought. He felt a sharp pain in his head. Then there was nothing.

People who were dining in the restaurant at the time began screaming in horror. Many of them ran for the exit. Like herd of stampeding Buffalo. Bumping into one another. Knocking other people to the floor. Who covered their heads. Trying to protect themselves as they were nearly trampled to death. By the fleeing masses. Others stopped to take pictures and videos on their smart phone's. Probably uploading them straight to facebook and Youtube. Only one person out of forty diners stopped and phoned the police.

Staring through the telescope mounted on his high powered sniper riffle. Raphael Monroe watched as events unfolded. In the diner half a mile away. The youth of today were clearly misled and disturbed. Recording the incident completely unfazed. They should be calling for help or running for the hills. Monroe had seen enough. It was time to go. He sat up from his sniping position and speedily took apart his riffle. It had being even easer than he had anticipated to lure the former Prime Minister out into the open. Pretending to be the kidnapper. Telling him that his daughter was going to be returned. He knew Harry would be so relived and happy about that news. That he wouldn't think things through. Wouldn't even waste time calling the police. No he would come straight out to meet his daughter. Right where Monroe wanted him to be. All he needed was a young girl as bait. To stand in for Amber. That proved easy enough to set up. As Jody Simm had an agent who had a similarly aged daughter.

They would both be disguised and sent back to America before anyone started looking for them. For now they were just face's in a crowd lost an forgotten.

Chapter eleven

The call had just come. A man matching Harry Worthington's description had been shot dead. Shot once in the head in the middle of a pizza restaurant. All witnesses had reportedly fled the scene. DCI Adam Greenhorn, DI Summer Richards and a fleet of uniform police officers were despatched to the scene immediately. Sirens Screeched as police car's sped down the streets at illegal speeds. Car's pulled up and stopped along the pavement. Outside the restaurant. Adam and Summer climbed out of their car and made their way to the front of the restaurant. While uniformed police officers were busy cording off the crime scene. With black and yellow hazard tape. If needed they would call for metal barriers. Adam knocked on the pizza place's door. Which was swiftly unlocked and opened by a rather shaken manager. "The body is just over there." The manger told Adam doing his best not to look at the dead man lying slumped in his restaurant.

"Where's the pathologist?" Adam asked.

"Should be here any minute now" Summer said as she glanced at her watch.

"Did anyone touch the body" Adam asked the Manager. Who looked desperate to get of there and go home.

"A couple of kids took pictures. You know how it is these days. But no one touched the body."

"Good" Adam replied. "Look I know this has been traumatic and you re probably keen to go home. But I'm afraid I need you to stick around and answer some questions. You feel up to that"

"I'll be ok." The manger didn't sound too sure. But his response was good enough for Adam. Who was also relieved to finally see his Pathologist at the crime scene.

"Good you're here" Adam said.

"I would have been here sooner but I had to park half a mile down the street" Kay said. Making reference to all the police cars parked in the vicinity.

"What have we got. Oh my God" Kay blurted out in shock. Clearly she wasn't expecting the victim to be the former Prime Minister, Harry Worthington. The gothic looking pathologist put her latex gloves on and started checking the body. She began by taking the bodies temperature. Then checking the bullet wound. Kay took mental notes as she went along. It had already been an uneasy promotion as it was. Taking over from her brutally murdered mentor. He had told her many time's that she was ready to step up. But Kay hadn't been convinced. Then out of nowhere she was thrown straight into the deep end. Working on a high profile case and now this. The former Prime Minister for goodness sakes.

"Bare in mind that with out ballistic reports and all my equipment. I doubt I can tell you much more than you already know."

"Indulge us" Adam insisted.

"I would say victim was shot by a high powered semi automatic Sniper Riffle. Which means the perpetrator could off been miles away. When he fired the shot. Taking into account. The accuracy of the shot. I would guess that this was a professional hit. No exit wound so at least the bullet is lodged in his head. Weather that will tell us much. Professional assassins usually use untraceable bullets."

"Great" Adam sighed. "I bet it was the bloody CIA. Obviously felt they had to keep Harry quiet. On a permanent basis. We will never catch the perpetrator. He will be long gone by now." Adam said angrily. "What about damage control."

"I think you can forget about that Sir" Summer said as she showed Adam a video on her iphone.

"Christ" Adam spat. As he watched a video showing the shot Harry Worthington.

"All this technology has made our jobs a bleeding nightmares. Can't keep anything under wraps anymore. The media probably know about every visit the Queen makes to the lavatory" Adam and Summer took the mangers statement while Kay and her forensic team carefully loaded the body onto a gurney be taken back the mortuary.

Things were rapidly going from bad to worse an unknown assailant had just killed Harry Worthington. Who was on his way to the mortuary in a body bag. The perpetrator could have shot him from over a mile away if he wanted. There was little hope of finding where he took the shot from. Even if they did he probably wore a disguise. Highly unlikely he would have been seen. Just another random face carrying a large bag. Maybe the bullet in the victim would tell him something but he wasn't hopeful. Professional killers were too good and clever to use bullets that could be traced back to a name. Or at least their real name. Adam could see Summer sat at her desk looking dejected. Adam walked into her small office. "Look there is nothing you can do right now. You might as well go home get some rest. It will be ten pm soon. Maybe we will have more to go on tomorrow"

"Maybe" The tone in her voice suggested she believed that as much as Adam did. Summer sighed heavily "Just can't get my head round this. Everything has just gone so wrong. This case just keeps unravelling in front of us. One of our main suspects has been assonated. Amber is still being held hostage and Our killer vampire is still out there somewhere."

"I know it's all gone to shit." Adam said trying not to sound too defeated. "But you just never know. Just go home for now and get some rest detective. That's an order." He gave her a warm smile. Right now it was all he could offer her.

Summer smiled back and decided to do as she was told. But as she prepared to leave the station the text alert on her smart phone Chimed. The message was from an unknown source. Summer tapped on her smart phone curious and read the message. Come Meet me. Alone I'm at the Winchester Arms. Spencer x. It was obviously a trap. But what she could do. If Spencer was now a vampire there was no telling what he would do if she didn't show. There was no choice she had to go straight there.

Summer tucked her berretta in the back of her jeans as she walked up to the entrance of the Winchester Arms. Strangely the place looked closed and all the lights were off. Summer had a very bad feeling, as she walked up to entrance and pushed on the door. It swung open. *Someone must be here then.* Summer mused. She made her way cautiously inside. The Detective thought she could see a figure leaning against the bar. It was too dark to see properly. She had to move in closer. "Spencer?" Summer called out. "Is that you" Her question was met with silence. "Spencer are you ok. Why did you text?" She tried once more. But nothing the figure at the bar stayed motionless. Summer walked slowly and deliberately towards the bar. She really wished she had brought her sword with her now. But a stake would have do to. As she got closer to the bar. Summer could see that the man leaning against it wasn't Spencer. In fact he wasn't even alive. "God damn it" She whispered under her breath.

"Do you like my present?" came a voice. Summer looked around but couldn't see anyone. *Where the hell is he.* "Why don't you show your self" Summer demanded "You scared.?" The question was answered by manic laughing.

"Very well, I can't keep my audience waiting" Spencer stepped out from the darkness that concealed him. He wore his demon face. All contorted and ridged at the brows. Long fangs showed as he smiled and his yellow eyes seemed to dance in the dim light. "I'm sorry I abandoned you" Summer apologised. Feeling more than a little guilty

"Don't be sorry dear. I'm not. This is the best thing that's ever happened to me. I'm faster, stronger and smarter than ever. The best part, is going to be right now killing you. The world renowned hunter. Well maybe that's going overboard a bit. But hey might as well big you up. I want decent bragging rights here."

"Your crazy"

"No" Spencer laughed "I'm a vampire"

"What if I kill you fist Summer told him angrily as she reached behind her to grab her gun. But Spencer was ready. He kicked the gun clean out of Summer's hand before she could even think about pulling the trigger. Before the detective could regain her composer Spencer grabbed her arm and sent her crashing against the wall. Summer hit the wall with a massive thud and crumpled to the floor. Clutching her forehead in agonising pain Summer tried to climb back to her feet. But Spencer was already standing over her. He was far stronger and faster than she had imagined.

"Lucius was so concerned about you!" The vampire spat. "I mean look at you. You're weak and pathetic. Your not even a match for me. You couldn't save Harry and you wont be able to save Amber. When we are done with her I will peel her skin. She will die a slow agonising death."

"Stop it" Summer protested. His taunting was starting to get under her skin. Spencer grabbed Summer by her hair and hauled her up to her feet. He opened his mouth ready to take a bite out of the detectives neck. But instead he felt a massive pain in his groin. Summer had Kicked him hard in the balls. The intense pain took Spencer by surprise. He dropped Summer and fell to his knees howling in agony. Now was Summer's chance. She had to think fast. Her mind in survival mode running on instinct. Summer ran to the bar and grabbed a bottle of alcohol and a lighter. As she turned around Spencer was already back to his feet and coming round the bar. "What good do you think that will do you?" He mocked.

Summer smashed the bottle over the vampires head And flicked on the lighter. The alcohol that now saturated Spencer's face ignited almost immediately. He fell to the floor rolling and screaming in agony. As the fire quickly spread down his body. "Burn you son of a bitch!" Summer sneered angrily before ruining out of the Pub. She quickly called the fire service before giving the pubs address but a false name. She sincerely hoped that the fire would be enough to finish Spencer off.

Summer sat in her home completely exhausted from her fight with Spencer. She had called Price ten minutes ago but it felt like hours she needed to talk to him. She needed more answers. She took a sip of water and took at large bite out of a thick cheese and ham sandwich. She felt like eating something more substantial. But felt too tired to start cooking a big supper. Finally the door bell rang. Summer pulled herself off her couch and answered the door. "Come in" She welcomed in the chirpiest voice she could muster.

"Don't mind if I do" Price smiled in return. "Why did you call me over?" Price asked.

"you cut right past the pleasantries don't you"

"You've been fighting, haven't you?"

"How did you guess" Came Summers sarcastic reply.

"The fact you like you have been through ten rounds with Mike Tyson and the big bruise on your forehead. Was also a bit of a giveaway."

"He was strong Price. Stronger than the vampires I fought off in the warehouse. I barley defeated him. I can't help wonder if the vampires have already come up with a formula to make themselves stronger."

"You did say that's why they had Amber. If Snyder had already developed a formula to cure Amber. It's not unthinkable that he could come up with another in short order. Might just be a matter of tweaking a few things here and there. But you also have to bare in mind Vampire's are like humans. In the respect that they come in all different shapes and sizes. Some will likely be stronger than others. Some will be faster. That's why you need the training and why you shouldn't go too far without your sword. Saying all that. It is unusual for a newly sired vampire to be so strong. We need to stop Lucius before they prefect a serum. Or we could end up facing an unstoppable army of vampire's. We may need to up your training schedule to prepare you better.

I don't want to sound like Gok Wan here. But you may want to re-think your what you dress sense. Wearing less restrictive clothing will improve your fighting technique. You need to wear cloths that won't hinder your flexibility. Foot wear that won't upset your balance. We must look at any little thing we can tweak to make you the best fighter you can be" Price explained. Summer nodded and smiled in agreement. A war was coming and she needed to be ready.

It was late now well past one o clock. But Raphael Monroe was still running on eastern standard time and was wide awake. It was also a good time to call Deputy Director Reece. Monroe counted the rings as he waited for the other end to be picked up. One . . . two . . . . three. He heard the line pick up.

"Hello" Came the Deputy directors gruff voice.

"Its Monroe Sir. We took out Harry Worthington and the lab but we couldn't find the sample."

"Damn it" Logan Reece didn't sound impressed.

"We need that blood sample agent. Ok change of plan is patient Zero still alive" "As far as I know Sir" Monroe answered but according to my Intel the vampires have her."

"You need to find away to extract her and bring her back here."

"Even if I could take her from the vampires how do I get her back to America.?" "You let me worry about that. Just get the girl. Or don't bother coming back at all." The phone went dead. Raphael knew that Reece wasn't kidding. He had to get the girl. He scrolled through his contact list and called Jody Simm.

"Hope this is a booty call. Ringing me at this hour" She said playfully.

"I'm afraid its business" He heard a sigh on the other end of the line.

I'm gonna need your help. Reece wants us to pull an extraction on Patient Zero" "Are you serious!? You know the vamps have her right"

"I know" Raphael said calmly. "But I've got a plan."

Adam Greenhorn was shocked and a little upset that one of his best detectives had decided to hand in her badge. "You sure I can't change your mind?" He asked diligently.

"I'm sorry. But I've explained why in my letter of resignation. I know the reason may sound strange and be hard to swallow."

"All makes sense to me." Adam said sarcastically "you're a vampire Hunter with a greater mission"

"See I knew you would understand." Summer replied with a cheeky grin. A grin Adam had to admit he was going to miss.

"You know their going to cover it all up don't you? Adam said. "Their already preparing their excuses and cover ups. it's a scary enough world already they say. Can't have people worried about creatures of the night. Could drive us all insane" "There probably right"

"Yeah probably. At least I still got you for another month. I will work you to the bone" Adam laughed

"I have no doubt you will"

Summer could here her phone going off. She had left it in her coat. By the time Summer had reached her coat in her office the phone had stopped ringing. A missed call from her mum and a voice message. She pressed on her phone to take her to voice mail. "Hi honey only me just wanted to see how you are" Her mother had never managed to work out texts. Summer rang her back. "Hi Mum. I'm doing ok I guess. "Only ok" was her mothers stern reply. Whether it was because she missed her Mum more than usual lately. Or because of the impending battle ahead. Summer felt a great need to be with her Mother . . . "Lets meet up for Coffee mum. We haven't done anything together for ages."

"That's because you always too busy working."

"I know Mum. I wish I had more free time. I really do. I've got an hour for dinner at twelve. Meet me at the coffee place near the station."

"How can I turn down quality time with my favourite daughter. I will see you there"

Three hours later they met at the coffee shop. Summer ordered two lattes one with extra cream for herself. She felt like she needed the pick me up. She also ordered a lemon cup cake for her and a piece of chocolate gateau for her mother. They sat on table in the corner of the small café out of the way of the hustle and bustle of everyone else. Look at them Summer thought to herself. Going about their lives not a clue what's going on around them.

"Are you ok dear" Linda asked her daughter.

"Huh Oh I'm fine"

"You seemed away with the fairy's"

"Sorry Mum stuff on my mind I guess."

"How is your case going?"

"Not so good I'm afraid. We still haven't caught the perpetrator. We got no clues or anything to go so far. This guy doesn't seem to make mistakes."

"I am sure he will. We all do eventually" Linda new her words carried little comfort but it was all she could offer for now. Summer changed the subject onto dad and old times. Not wanting to tell her mum about quitting the force. She wouldn't believe the reasons why any way. Luckily her mum seemed oblivious to all the stories about vampires. Because Summer had no idea how she would explain that one. Linda smiled and placed her hand on Summer's "I know we always say this. Every time we see each other" She told her daughter "But we should do this more often." "Definitely" Summer agreed. "I love you Mum" Summer felt the need to say it. Almost as if she didn't expect to survive the impending battle.

PART FOUR

Why We Fight

Chapter twelve

News reached Lucius that Spencer had been killed by the hunter. Burnt to a crisp. Inside the very pub he had hopped to trap her in. If he was unable to defeat the hunter then the serum still wasn't affective enough. He would have to give Snyder more time to refine and perfect his formula. In the meantime Lucius was sure the Hunter would come back to the warehouse. She would want to save the girl if nothing else. But the old vampire would be ready for her. He had men on the doors and if she managed to get past them. Well she wouldn't be the first Hunter he would of faced and outlived. If Summer came here looking for Amber. She would find only death.

This was it. Summer would go in tonight. She couldn't risk going in all guns blazing. She would have to use stealth. Sneak up on her enemy and kill them quickly and silently. Getting Amber out of there in one piece was her number one priority. Any vamps she missed could be tracked down and killed another day. Taking Price's advice Summer decided to dress herself in a black t shirt, thick black leggings, black boots with a normal heel, a sash around her waist to hold her sword in place and of coarse her black rain coat. Summer also tied red locks back into a tight pony tail. In the pockets of her coat she hid a couple of wooden stakes. Summer was ready for battle.

Giles Price drove Summer as near to the warehouse as they dared. Any sound could alert the vampires to their presence. Especially the rumble of a cars engine. Price would wait in the car as back up just in case. But Summer would need to go the rest of the way alone and on foot. To ensure she remained undetected. Summer knew that Lucius would have all the doors guarded. No doubt he would be expecting her. Summer needed to find another way in. keeping to the shadows as she approached the warehouse she looked for an alternative entrance. She looked up to see a window on the second floor. There was no real way of getting to it and what if it was locked shut. No this wasn't an action movie, there must be a better way. As she walked round to the front of the building she saw a small hole on the floor. Probably where an air vent used to be. Maybe she could squeeze her slender frame through there. Summer got down on her belly and pulled her self through the gap in the wall. It was pitch black inside the warehouse. But The Hunters eyes quickly adjusted. Must *be one of my new abilities* Summer thought. She stayed crouched down in the same spot for several minuets.

Trying to take in her surroundings. Looking and listening for any movement. There it was to her left. A vampire watching an entrance. The demon seemed totally focused on watching the door. Satisfied she could sneak up on him Summer crept over to the vampire's position. Quickly and silently she drew her Katana. With one swift and silent movement she brought her sword round slicing through the monsters neck. The razor sharp blade cut through the vampire guards flesh and bone like butter. He was nothing more than a pile of ash on the floor. Summer had to reach the offices upstairs. That's where Lucius would be holding Amber. That's where he would be waiting. As Summer made her way to the metal stairs she took out another vamp. Just as swiftly and quietly as the first. The more she killed now the less she would have fight, once they were alerted to her presence. Summer got to the metal stairs case. She thought she saw movement at her eleven o clock in the shadows. She held her gaze for several seconds. Concentrating, listening. There was nothing there. Just her imagination. Summer crept up the stairs slowly, keeping her head down. She didn't want to be seen just yet. *Strange.* Summer thought. As she realised there where no vamps stationed on the top of the stairs. Maybe they didn't think she would get this far. Or more likely it was a trap. Summer could see two doors on this second floor. But she had no idea which one to enter. No idea what lay in wait behind either door. There was only one thing for it. Summer drew her Katana and held it at the ready.

She walked up to the first door and kicked it open. Three vampires lay in wait to ambush her. A quick swing of her sword brought it down to two. But as she attacked a second vampire. A third grabbed her from behind. Hooking his arms through hers and holding her firm at the back of the neck. Summer lost her grip on the sword and it clattered onto the floor. As one vampire held her. The other Vampire came in for the kill. He was smiling manically as he walked towards Summer fangs baring. The Hunter kicked out aiming high. Her foot connected with the vamps face and he staggered backward. Out muscling the vampire that held her Summer broke free. In what seemed like a split second. Summer grabbed a stake from her coat pocket span herself round and plunged the stake into the vampires heart. Summer fell forward catching herself with her hands. She swivelled round on the floor kicking the last vampires ankles and sweeping him off his feet. Stake still in hand she drove it into the vamps chest before he could get back up.

So Amber was in the next room. That also meant Lucius would be too. Summer dusted herself off and picked up her sword. She walked out of the room and towards door number two. Before she got there, Lucius burst threw the door and onto the walkway. He was dressed in a smart black suit and held a katana of his own.

"This belonged to one of your ancestors" The vampire smiled. "She begged for her life before I killed her."

"There will be no begging tonight" Summer said defiantly.

"We will just have to see about that" The vampire hissed. Lucius walked methodically towards Summer. He was different to the other vampires. He had an air about him, confidence and a superiority. He acted like Summers death was inevitable. Summer hopped that his confidence was misplaced. The vampire swung his sword ruthlessly at Summer going straight for the kill. But she brought her sword up and blocked his attack. The force of the blow stunned Summer and forced back. This vampire was strong. Seeing his opponent stagger back. Lucius brought his sword round again. Once again the Hunter parried the shot. But took several more steps backwards. Again steal clashed against steal as the vampire kept ups his attack. This time a wicked smile crept across his face. Realising where she was Summer knew why. But it was too late. The vampire lashed out with a kick that connected with Summers sternum. She fell crashing down the stairs. Rolling all the way down and dropping her sword along the way.

"You're a fool" Lucius said as he stalked down the stair case after her. "Coming here thinking you could be a match for me." Summer didn't respond. She was battered and bruised but climbed to her feet non the less. Arming herself with the only weapon she had left, her wooden stake. She held her ground at the bottom of the stair case and stared hard into Lucius's cold yellow eyes. He swung his sword at Summer's neck as he reached the bottom of the stair case. But she dodged out of the way at the last second. The vampire cursed as he lost his balance momentarily. Summer sent in a kick knocking the katana out of the vampires hand. The blade clattered to the floor and slid out of view into the shadows. Now they where even.

"I don't need a sword to defeat you anyway" Lucius taunted. As he threw a strong right hook which Summer blocked. She threw a punch of her own with her free hand but her attempt was blocked as well. Summer was then knocked back by a hard head butt. She thought she saw movement behind Lucius but was too dazed to be sure. Lucius landed another blow and then another. Summer staggered back before falling to one knee.

"Why do you fight for these people" Lucius asked his helpless opponent. "They are so vain and arrogant. Their greed for money and power is only outstripped by their stupidity. Humans will undoubtedly destroy this planet and everything on it"

"I fight Because no matter how bad you paint the human race. Your kind will always be far worse" Summer retorted as she wiped away blood from her mouth.

"Do you honestly believe that?" The vampire scoffed. "My kind will be reborn under a new rule" Lucius insisted as he aimed a kick towards Summer's face. She caught the demons foot and twisted it round as she stood up. The vampire fell sprawling to the floor. Summer took a second to compose herself as Lucius quickly rose to his feet. Summer stood still almost daring Lucius to continue his attack. He threw several punch's all of which failed to connect with his intended target. She wasn't even trying to fight anymore. The tactic seemed to baffle the vampire as he fruitlessly attempted to strike the Hunter. The tactic was working the vampire was becoming visibly frustrated. Lucius sent in another blow, this time Summer caught his wrist and struck with a palm heel strike. The blow landed just under the vampires chin, snapping his head back sharply. Summer followed up with flurry of solid punches to the vampires face and mid-section. She followed up with a hard kick to the knee. The vampires leg buckled and he fell to the floor. Summer wasted no time. She sent a massive round house kick crashing against the vampires skull. Lucius fell flat on the floor. Summer mounted the vampire. Using her legs to pin his arms to the floor. Clutching her stake in both hands she pressed it against Lucius's chest. Right above his heart. The vampire laughed and evil maniacal laugh.

"You think you have won" he sniggered

"You think this is the end. But I am only the beginning. I thought I was going to lead a new vampire kingdom. But there are others far worse than me. I am just a martyr. A darkness is coming and with it all light will be extinguished. Even yours."

"Not before your dust!" Summer told him before pushing the stake into the demons chest. In a second he was gone. As Summer climbed to her feet and turned around she saw two figures running to the door. One of them appeared to be carrying someone.

It was Amber, Summer was sure of it what the hell was going on.

Across the street from the warehouse two silhouettes watched from their hiding place. Dressed in full tactical gear and watching every movement through infra red goggles. Agents Raphael Monroe and Jody Simm waited. They would have to be patient, but they also had to be ready. Their window of opportunity could come and go at a moments notice. They had just once chance to get this right.

"You sure she is going to come?" Jody Simm asked getting inpatient.

"She will come." Monroe ensured her. "Your mole in the police department said this is where the vampire is holding the girl. Our patient Zero. If they want to save her they will have to act in the next two or three nights. It will be a special ops mission. Strictly stealth. They will send Two Maybe three operatives to extract her. We wait for them to show. Then follow them in but keeping our distance. When everyone is distracted we go in and get the girl.

"You make it sound so simple" Simm snipped.

"It is in theory. But pulling it off will be tricky."

"hang on a second what's that at seven o clock" Simm pointed out. Raphael looked in the direction Simm had mentioned. Through his infra red goggles he could see a lone person running the perimeter of the warehouse.

"Is that it, their only sending in one person" Simm asked puzzled.

"Looks like" Raphael responded un fazed.

"What aren't you telling me" Simm demanded "Not now. Looks like She's found away in lets go." Monroe and Simm made there way slowly across the street. Once at the warehouse Monroe peered through a window. He could see the heat signature of the special operative and a figure that registered at room temperature. A vampire. A second later the vampire was gone. "Quick over here through the door." Monroe ordered "Are you crazy" Simm responded as she followed closely behind.

"Trust me. Just stay close." "Monroe took out his Glock. That he had already fitted with a suppressor and fired two shots at the lock on the door. The bullets shattered the old, decaying locks of the warehouse door. Enabling Monroe to push it open. Keeping low and to the shadows. The two agents crept inside making their way to the buildings stair case. They had both memorized the warehouse's schematics before starting their mission. Monroe held up his fist instructing Simm to stop dead. He had been seen he was sure of it. He could feel the eyes of the other operative boring right through him. Just as Monroe thought the mission was over. The operative carried on their way. *That was too close* he thought. As they waited a few more moments before proceeding towards the stair case. As they got to the cold metal stairs of the warehouse he could see the other operative entering a room on the second floor.

"We may to engage the other operative to collect the package" Monroe whispered. "We can wait over here. Take him by surprise." Agent Monroe found a suitable place were they could hide unseen and watch events unfold. They would only engage the other operative if necessary. The package had to be delivered intact. The agents waited in the darkness for several minutes before the other operative walked out of the room. Empty handed. Someone else appeared on the upper walkway. It was another vampire. Monroe watched as the vampire and operative engaged in battle. Raphael couldn't help but wonder who this person was. That could go toe to toe with a vampire. Could the operative be the Demon Hunter. He had heard about. He could of sworn that was just the stuff of legend. But then again that's what most people thought about vampires. The vampire seemed to be getting the upper hand in the battle. But Raphael needed the two combatants to move away from the stair case. Before he could make his move. It looked like his prayers had been answered as the operative came crashing down the stair case. The vampire followed its opponent down and carried on with the battle.

"Now" Monroe ordered. As he made a brake for it. The fight looked like it was nearly over but this was their best chance to slip by unnoticed. They quickly moved up the stairs and approached the far door. There was no time to be cautious. Monroe kicked the door open. The room looked as if it had been turned in a make shift lab. With only the package and a sole vampire inside. Before the vampire had a chance to react to the two intruders. Agent Simm fired a high voltage taser gun. The taers's probes lodged into the vampires chest. As with a human the vampire lost all control of his nervous system. He fell to a shuddering heap on the floor. Simm squeezed the trigger of the taser increasing the voltage and intensifying the shock. Making sure the vampire stayed grounded. While Simm kept the vampire busy, Monroe took out a small knife and cut Amber free of her bonds. He picked her up from the table and threw her over his shoulder.

They ran out of the room and back down the stairs. The two agents didn't even see Summer killing Luicus as they made their escape. They ran trough the door and outside into to moonlit night.

"We've been made" Simm said worried. "There's a female operative about one hundred meters behind us"

"We're nearly at the car keep going" They raced across the street and to a black Land Rover Discovery. They opened the doors and threw the girl in the back. Monroe jumped into the drivers seat and Simm got in the back with the girl. Monroe started the engine and pulled away just as Summer got to the discovery. She tried to hold on to the passenger door. But was forced to let go as the Land Rover pulled away at speed. She stood and watched helpless as the black Discovery disappeared round a corner.

Summer jumped, startled by the car pulling up beside her. Almost knocking her down. "Get in" Price shouted. But Summer was already opening the passenger door. Tyres screeched as Price drove off at high speed. "I decided to come a bit closer to the warehouse in case you needed a quick get away." Price explained

"Can't fault your timing" Summer smiled. "What happened?" Price asked keeping his eyes firmly on the road.

"Turns out some one else wants Amber" "Probably the Americans" Price suggested. "Could be anyone." Summer added Who knows what's really going on and who's involved. That's the car" Summer pointed at the black Discovery that was five cars ahead. "Where do you think their heading"? Summer asked.

"Best Guess an air strip. They will be looking to get her out of the country as quick as possible I would say"

"We can't let that happen"

"And we won't." A determined price assured her. He pressed down on the accelerator and began weaving through traffic. Drivers made rude gestures and blew their horns as Price cut them up and got a little too close for comfort more than once. But he knew he had to throw caution to the wind. They had to catch up with the kidnappers. They would probably have small private plane ready for take off. Waiting at the air strip. The Discovery made a sudden turn at a red light. Cars slid and collided with each other. Causing a small pile up and almost blocking the way.

"No!" Summer cried.

"Hold on" Price ordered as he mounted a curb to avoid the pile up. He turned hard left to follow the Discovery.

"We've lost them" Summer panicked as the discovery seemed to be no where in site. "No we haven't. there's only one place their heading. They just turned off to throw us. We will catch them up in a minute." Sure enough Price was right. As they joined the motor way they could see the Land Rover and it was now only two cars ahead. But they obviously knew they were being pursued As the vehicle suddenly sped up. Price put his foot down in response. They were doing over a hundred mile per hour now. But still not gaining. Without indicating the car suddenly left the motor way. Horns blew from frustrated drivers. Followed by more as Price cut across in hot pursuit. They chased the discovery for four miles gaining on it every second. They were less than a car length away before the four by four veered off down a rough looking piece of road. The road was narrow and bumpy. Better suited to the Discovery than a sporty Audi TT. Just slightly ahead now the Discovery pulled up. A man got out from the drivers side and a woman came out of the back carrying Ambers arm. They raced across the tarmac to the waiting plane. Price stopped and Summer jumped out. "Stop Police!" She Screamed as she ran as fast as she could. Amber managed to struggle free and fell to the ground. forcing the agent holding her to loose her balance and fall too. Summer could hear sirens in distance As she ran towards the fallen girl.

There was a loud bang and summer felt a searing pain in her chest. Suddenly she couldn't breath. She fell to her knees clutching her wound and gasping for air. Price ran to her side. Firing a gun of his own at the two agents. It seemed the female agent had forgot about Amber as she ran towards the plane. But seeing Price with a gun Monroe had already boarded and called for take off. Jody Simm Screamed and cursed at the moving plane. The sirens screamed loudly now as the police pulled up onto the air strip. Jody Simm knew the jig was up. She would be left to take the blame alone. Summer was lying on the floor still struggling for breath. "Your going be ok" Price assured her. "Don't panic. It will hurt like hell. But it looks as if the bullet has missed anything vital." But Summer was in too much pain to think. All she could see was spots so she closed her eyes and let everything fade to darkness.

When Summer came round everything was a blur. She could hear chatter around her. But couldn't focus. Gradually she started to recognized voices. Face's started to become clear. She knew exactly where she was. Hospital. A drip was connected to her hand and she also seemed to be connected to a heart monitor. She tried to sit up but it took too much effort. "Relax" Came the familiar voice of her Mother Linda. "You've been through quite an ordeal."

"How long was I out" Summer managed to ask.

"Two days" Price answered. "You were shot in the chest. Thankfully the bullet missed your vitals."

"What about the girl"

"Amber was shaken and hungry" But other than that ok. Apart from taking samples of her blood. The kidnappers didn't appear to harm her. She will be taken into protective custody. And then to a loving family" Price told her. "You just need to concentrate on your own recovery"

"Mr Price is right" Linda told her daughter.

"Try not to worry. They caught the kidnapper after all. Some American fanatic. She will be going to prison for a long time"

So that was the yarn they were spinning. Summer knew there was more to it than that. The woman had at least one ally. CIA Summer suspected. They had probably severed all ties with her now. Thrown her to the lions as a scapegoat. Summer almost felt sorry for the woman she was probably only following orders after all.

A week later Summer was discharged from hospital. Doctors had been astounded by her fast recovery. In fact she had felt ready to leave two days earlier. But doctors had been reluctant to let her go. Price had told her that as a Hunter her body would heal far faster than that of a normal human. It was probably the reason she was still alive. He still couldn't be certain why the Powers had activated her as a Hunter. But he had a feeling the reasons would become clear soon enough. *Maybe a new age of magic was dawning* he had pondered. Or maybe more evil was afoot. Whatever the case Summer had quit the force. She would now be focusing on her training.

Focusing on her new life as a Hunter. Her life had changed and things were only going to get stranger.

Epilouge

Alice Holiday sat in her knew office. It was still empty apart from the large oak desk. Left by her predecessor. Which she was sure she would keep. Be time to move her things in on the weekend. Then there was the chore of moving into her new home. Still it will all be worth it. Things had gone quickly but not totally unexpectedly. Alice was lost in thought when the sound of her phone ringing brought her back to reality. She looked at the screen. It read Caller ID Withheld. Alice decided to answer the phone anyway.

"I just rang to offer my congratulations." came the familiar American tones on the other line. "We have an exciting new future on the horizon. I also want to thank you on a job well done. Pinning the death of Harry Worthington and the kidnapping of his daughter on Jody Simm."

"We wouldn't of been able to do that without the evidence the CIA provided me with." Alice admitted

"Still a job well done. We got the blood samples of Patient Zero. Which will be very useful and we received your package. Blood from the Demon Hunter. Should make for some fascinating research. How did you procure it?"

"Lets just say I have my people in the hospital"

"Ha" the American laughed. "We will also have the girl aka Patient Zero under constant surveillance and observation. We will also keep a good eye on the Demon Hunter too. Lucius was old and strong. But the Hunter killed him non the less. We shouldn't underestimate her"

"Agreed We will be monitoring things from our end too. Do you think Lucius had any idea who he was going against?"

"If he did he obviously thought he could use Patient Zero as leverage"

"It's of no consequence now. Once again you have my sincere. Congratulations, Prime Minister."

"Thank you Mr President."

The End